ALIEN SPECTATORS

By Donald W. Desaulniers

Table of Contents

ABOUT THE AUTHOR

Donald W. Desaulniers is a Canadian lawyer who
operated his own legal practice in the
beautiful small city of Belleville, Ontario
from 1973 until he retired in 2009. He is a
graduate of University of Waterloo (1968) and
University of Western Ontario Law School
(1971). Still residing in Belleville with his
lovely English wife, Jane and their one

remaining cat, the author has published more
than eighty novels, all of which are available
on Amazon as either E-Books or in paperback
form.

NOVELS ABOUT LAWYERS

DISCARDED LAWYER (But Not Dead Yet)
LOCKDOWN LAWYER
SHUT THAT LAWYER UP
FAILED LAWYER, POMPOUS ANGEL
LUCKY LAWYER
PARADE OF DEAD LAWYERS
THE LORD SNATCHES AWAY
LOATHING THE LAWYER, LOVING THE LAWYER
LADY LUCK LOVES LAWYERS
THE CHRISTMAS LAWYER
FIFTY YEARS LATER (Hitchhiking in Donald
Trump's America)
REVENGE DELAYED
TEMPTING THE GOOD LALWYER
TERRORIST LAWYER
THE LAWYER'S MUSLIM NEIGHBORS
RICH LAWYER, POOR PRIEST
FAKE LAWYER
NAÏVE LAWYER
BUYING REDEMPTION
LAWYER IN THE TOILET

SLIMY LAWYER (#1 in Series)
SLIMY SUES AMERICA (#2 in Series)
SLIMY GETS SHAFTED (#3 in Series)
SLIMY GETS DISBARRED (#4 in Series)
SLIMY TASTES THE GOOD LIFE (#5 in Series)
SLIMY LAWYER CHECKS OUT (#6 in Series)

THE WRONG LAWYER (#1 in Series)
SNARKY LAWYERS (#2 in Series)

VANISHING LAWYER (A WORLD WITHOUT ME)
VANISHING LAWYER #2 (UNWANTED WITNESS)
VANISHING LAWYER #3 (FUGITIVE ALIEN)
VANISHING LAWYER #4 (SAVING THE PRESIDENT)
VANISHING LAWYER #5 (SWINDLING SENIORS)
VANISHING LAWYER #6 (SAVING TRUMP AGAIN)

WEIRD LAWYER #1 (NOVICE ATTORNEY)
WEIRD LAWYER #2 (TOUGH TIMES)
WEIRD LAWYER #3 (A PINCH OF JEALOUSY)

ACTION NOVELS

DIVERGENT LAWYER
ALIEN SPECTATORS
DIE NOW OLD MAN
VILE FAMILIES
THE LEFT TACKLE'S CHRISTMAS
CROSSING A RICH MAN (Turning the Tables)
ESCAPE FROM EVERYTHING
MARTY MARCOTTE'S REVOLVING LIFE

TY WARD HITS AMERICA (#1 in Series)
TY WARD'S HOLIDAY FROM HELL (#2 in Series)
TY WARD'S NEXT WAR (#3 in Series)
DEADLY WITNESS (#4 in Series)
A YOUNG HOOKER'S THANKS (#5 in Series)
TY WARD'S LAST WAR (#6 in Series)
TY WARD'S SHATTERED PEACE (#7 in Series)
TY WARD'S ROUGH JUSTICE (#8 in Series)

WARD JONES #1 (Fledgling Predator)
WARD JONES #2 (Damsels in Distress)

NON-FICTION ESSAYS

CANADA'S FISCAL INSANITY (And Loss of
Freedoms)

ADVICE TO STUDENTS FROM AN OLD FART (Surviving University)

YOUNG ADULT NOVELS

MYSTERY OF THE OLD DESK
YOUNG BUT NOT STUPID
REVENGE DELAYED
CELESTIAL COINCIDENCE

NOVELS WITH ROMANTIC THEMES

BEVY OF BEAUTIES (Finding Love After Loss)
SWEET ROMANCE BACK HOME
LOVE SAVES A LONER
LOVE SEDUCES A FOOL
THE LIPPY LAWYER'S ROMANCE
BROKE, DISGRACED AND ALONE
THE CHEAPSKATE TWINS
A RETIRED LAWYER'S DOOMED ROMANCE

NOVELS WRITTEN UNDER PEN NAME LANCE MAJESTIK

UNDERCOVER TRUCKER (An American Mystery)
BETTER TIMES (A Comeback Story)
OLD MIND, YOUNG BODY (BODY SWITCH)
LOVE IN OLEAN (An American Romance)
CRAZY OLD LAWYER (A Talking Skin Tag)
LOVE MOCKS A LIMP DICK (War of the Sexes)

NOVELS WRITTEN UNDER PEN NAME DURWARD GARBAGE

WRONG PLACE, WORST TIME
ABANDONED ALIEN (Space Aliens for Donald
Trump)
GOLDEN CHAOS (Stock Market Meltdown)
NASTY MAN (Mr. Jerk)
ALMOST A LAWYER
SQUANDERING MY FORTUNE

REVENGE FROM HER GRAVE
LAWYER ON THE RUN (Panhandling Attorney)
SCORNFUL FAMILY (Eating Insults)

CHAPTER 1 (Freak Lawyer)

I'm some weird freak of nature.

My name is Ronald Smith and I look like a normal healthy guy of sixty-four. I'm roughly six feet tall, slender with only the earliest hint of a tiny beer gut, and I sport a full crop of sandy colored hair slightly peppered with touches of grey.

My strange uniqueness is entirely mental.

I was a retired attorney in the small Canadian city of Belleville, Ontario where I resided with my late wife, Hannah who passed away ten years ago in 2005.

I retired slightly more than two years ago in 2012 but quickly got bored. My best friend had died before I packed in my legal practice and I really didn't have any other close friends. Retirement threw me completely out of the loop and I no longer had anyone to meet for lunch or otherwise hang around with.

To alleviate that boredom I did something completely out of character and entirely daring. I left Belleville and moved to a depressed city in southwestern Ontario called Laughlin where I rented an apartment in a century-old tenement building that once had been an orphanage.

My goal apparently was to live among the poor and learn about them. Despite the fact that I was quite wealthy, I was also a deplorable cheapskate and hated to spend money.

I took a "job" washing dishes in a disgusting bums' hotel for no pay, again for the alleged reason of observing the destitute of society in a strange quest to understand what made them tick.

The reason I'm using terms like "apparently" and "alleged" is at the core of my freakiness.

I don't remember a damn thing about any of it.

I was robbed and mugged in Laughlin on March 23rd by the very scum I was trying to study and I fell into a coma.

I now call that fellow "Old Ron" and refer to myself as "New Ron."

I awoke from that coma on March 25th but with no recollection of the previous sixty-four years while Old Ron roamed the planet.

My general knowledge remained intact which meant that I remembered how to drive, cook and do pretty much everything else. It was only the specific memories which I lost. I don't remember anything much about being a lawyer and absolutely nothing about my late wife and my many years with her.

I learned about Old Ron's life by reading his diaries which I found in his apartment.

Oddly, the new me retained no vestiges of the insane frugality that permeated every bone in Old Ron's body.

I believed that money was meant to be spent and enjoyed.

When I emerged from the coma and discovered what a disgusting cheapskate I'd been, I couldn't get out of Laughlin fast enough. I scored some easy money from the newspaper and police department which had mishandled Old Ron in every way imaginable. The cops assumed incorrectly that he was a passed-out drunk and didn't bother to check him for injuries, and the paper ran a scathing story smearing Old

Ron as a disgraced drunken shyster. They paid me off to avoid an embarrassing lawsuit.

I gave Old Ron's 2002 Chevrolet Cavalier to his landlady, and used some of the lawsuit settlement to buy myself a brand new Cadillac CTS touring sedan. Immediately thereafter I escaped Old Ron's life of poverty by embarking on a driving trip.

On the very first night of that journey I met a lovely woman named Sonia Poniecki in the fancy hotel in Chicago called the Rushmore Arms where I had taken a suite for three nights.

Over the ensuing week we fell in love whereupon Sonia agreed to join me on my travelling adventure.

We meandered blissfully around a healthy chunk of America before eventually winding up in Las Vegas.

We booked a suite for three nights in the Metropolis, the newest strip mega resort and we were having a marvelous time together.

During some terrifying turbulence on a helicopter tour returning from the Grand Canyon, I hit my head hard against the window. The accident must have scrambled my brain because that's when the trouble began.

Old Ron and I started to meet in shared dreams.

The cheapskate and I instantly loathed one another because we had such vastly different outlooks on life and money.

As if that wasn't upsetting enough, we didn't know which version of Ron Smith would emerge on any given morning.

Old Ron had popped out with Sonia the morning after our first shared dream. Coincidentally that was the morning when our reservation at the Metropolis was set to expire. As I learned later, Old Ron was so shocked at the price of the room there that he coerced Sonia to move downtown to the El Cortez, a budget hotel and casino where Old Ron had often stayed on his previous trips to Las Vegas.

On subsequent days when I emerged, Sonia had persuaded me to remain at the El Cortez because all of the shared dreams took place in Room 321 there.

It was a difficult situation for poor Sonia who grew to love us both although for the life of me, I couldn't comprehend why she tolerated the insane thrift cheerfully practised by that hopeless cheapskate.

Two days ago while I was the one in the real world with Sonia, she received a call on her BlackBerry that her father, Cecil had suffered a serious stroke back in Chicago and was in intensive care. Sonia flew home that very night and I promised her that Old Ron and I would drive immediately to Chicago to join her. I foolishly assured her that the miser and I would have no difficulty putting aside our childish acrimony and that Old Ron and I could communicate with each other by leaving detailed notes setting out where the car was located and what was on the agenda for the next day. I also comforted Sonia that Old Ron and I would also fill each other in on the previous day's events in our shared dreams so that it really didn't matter which one of us emerged on any given morning.

Based on those calm assurances, Sonia flew back home to be at her Dad's bedside.

How was I to know that the all-encompassing abhorrence that Old Ron and I felt for each other would create an impossible impediment to cooperation and effective communication?

Sure enough, I made the mistake of leaving a terse note that first night telling Old Ron simply to drive to Grand Junction, Colorado on Wednesday morning. I had expected to tell the miser the whole story about Cecil's stroke in our nightly dream.

Instead, the intense rivalry and distrust got in the way the moment we met in our dream on Tuesday night, and we immediately began arguing about an adolescent prank Old Ron had pulled the previous day when he hid my Cadillac.

Old Ron jumped to the erroneous conclusion that Sonia had left Las Vegas because of some terrible argument with me, and I was unable to set the record straight before our dream abruptly ended.

When we squared off again in dreamland last night, I learned to my disgust that Old Ron had totally ignored my written instructions and that we were still in Las Vegas.

In absolute rage I issued a challenge in an attempt to settle our differences once and for all. It was intolerable sharing my life and my beloved Sonia with such an impossible stubborn miser.

We peeled ourselves off our respective dream clouds and slowly and painstakingly forced our dream bodies to meet in the center of this hotel room at the El Cortez in a fight to the finish.

All I can remember about the battle itself was my fist, arm and then right shoulder getting absorbed into Old Ron's angry face as I delivered a slow-motion punch to his disgusting mug.

It was somewhat reassuring that I was the Ron Smith waking up on the carpet today, but the full import of my reappearance wasn't yet decipherable.

I fervently hoped that I'd seen the last of Old Ron.

One aspect of our recent prize fight was apparent. We hadn't merged into one entity because I still had no recollection of the period prior to waking up in the Laughlin hospital. I also still retained my firm belief that money was meant to be enjoyed, not hoarded.

I looked around the room. Something didn't add up.

CHAPTER 2 (What Just Happened?)

I was definitely still at the El Cortez. The bed had clearly been slept in because the sheets and blanket were bunched up in total disarray.

I stood up, clad just in my underwear, and tried to get my bearings.

My watch was on the nightstand beside the king-size bed. I walked over and checked the time.

The timepiece showed that today was Thursday, May 7th, 2015 which meant that I had missed all day Wednesday. That confirmed what I'd discovered in last night's dream. Old Ron had occupied reality yesterday.

The time shown on both my watch and the small radio clock on the nightstand was seven o'clock which made sense because I had just woken up.

I pulled open the heavy window drapes and looked out at a clear blue sky overhead, but something was wrong.

Normally the sunlight would be blaring into the room at this time of morning because of the direction the windows faced, but at this moment the sun wasn't even visible.

Still not fully in command of my faculties, I called the front desk.

"Sorry to bother you, but I just woke up. Can you tell me what time it is and when my room reservation expires?"

"Of course, sir, let's see. You're paid up until tomorrow at noon and the time at this moment is two minutes past seven."

"Forgive my confusion, but is it morning or evening right now?"

14

The clerk chuckled.

"I guess you had a pretty rough night, sir. That's why people come to Las Vegas. It's Thursday evening. Is there anything else I can help you with?"

"Thank you, but not at this time," I answered as I put the receiver back in its cradle.

I sat down on the bed to collect my thoughts.

Did my having slept all bloody day have any significance?

Although my main priority remained getting my sorry carcass to Chicago as quickly as possible, I felt too fragile to pack my bags and hit the road at such a late hour. It would be getting dark in the next hour or two so I wouldn't even be able to make it as far as Mesquite by nightfall.

Besides that, I was starving so I quickly showered and headed downstairs to the casino coffee shop to fill my growling stomach and come up with some reasonable plan of action.

It was half past eight when I returned to my Room 321. My journey to Chicago was encountering one roadblock after another. A full day had been lost yesterday because Old Ron at his exasperatingly frugal worst decided that the hotel was prepaid for a couple more nights so he stayed put rather than be charged for a room he didn't use.

Now today was also shot because of my inexplicable oversleeping. I decided to phone Sonia and try to explain why I was still stuck in Las Vegas.

That endeavor proved to be one frustrating dry well after another.

My first call was to Sonia's condominium, but it just kept ringing with no opportunity to leave a message. Because of our driving trip, Sonia had disabled her answering machine. It was apparent that she hadn't yet hooked it back up.

Next I tried calling Sonia's parents but it also rang on and on with no answering machine kicking in. Bernice and Cecil abhorred technology and refused to pay for call display or an answering device, and they never purchased or wanted a computer.

Finally I called information and asked for the phone number of Sonia's daughter and son-in-law, Karen and Jeff Chandler. A voice recording informed me that the number was unlisted. Jeff was a doctor in Chicago so I attempted to obtain his work number, but that was equally futile. Jeff worked in some sort of specialized clinic and wasn't individually listed.

Embarrassingly, I couldn't recall the surname of Sonia's other daughter, Nancy.

Old Ron's laptop computer had died a few days earlier so it was useless. I resolved to find some sort of internet café on my travels tomorrow in order to email Sonia.

Because of the two hour time difference, it would be too late to try the numbers again in an hour. Hopefully I'd have better luck tomorrow.

Sonia wouldn't think to contact me here at the El Cortez because as far as she knew, I'd left Las Vegas yesterday morning.

I packed most of my belongings into the suitcase and carried it to my car in the parking garage. That provided the first piece of solid good news. The Cadillac was exactly where I'd left it on Tuesday evening. Old Ron had hidden my vehicle in a failed schoolboy prank on Monday, not comprehending that quality automobiles came equipped with a GPS system. Once I'd realized that my car was missing, it took one simple phone call to discover its whereabouts. Fortunately, the idiot hadn't moved the car yesterday.

I decided to hit the sack and try to get an early start tomorrow. Despite my earlier marathon sleep, I felt quite tired even though I'd only been up and about for three hours.

Just in case Old Ron and I continued to alternate our days in reality, I left a detailed note explaining precisely why Sonia had flown to Chicago, where the car was now, and why I hadn't left today to join Sonia. I also mentioned that I'd been unable to contact anyone in Chicago.

CHAPTER 3 (Vanishing Cadillac)

When I woke back up, it was half past six
and this time as I threw open the curtains,
intense blinding sunlight flooded the room. I
knew it was morning.

My note to Old Ron was still on the
nightstand and my watch showed that today was
Friday, May 8th, which meant that it was me
waking up two days in a row. That pleased me
greatly.

Sharing time in the real world with Captain
Frugal had become a dreadful inconvenience and
source of anger, especially because my
counterpart had been having sex with Sonia at
every opportunity. That had made me damn
jealous.

I showered and packed my remaining
belongings into my small sports bag.

As I checked out of the hotel and signed
the credit card slip, my lips curled into a
self-satisfied smile. I had cleverly prepaid
the room using Old Ron's replacement credit
card which I had obtained shortly after waking
up in the Laughlin hospital. The detective
investigating the mugging had cancelled the
cheapskate's original card as soon as he
discovered that the lowlifes who mugged Old
Ron and left him on the cold sidewalk for
dead, had then used his credit card later that
evening to feast on an expensive meal
including copious bottles of beer.

Since I was in Las Vegas, I decided to cash
my remaining traveler's checks here at the
casino since it wasn't always easy to cash
them while on the move.

18

Still not entirely confident that I had sufficient funds in the event of some roadside emergency, I went to a cash machine in the casino and obtained $3,000 through the credit card. I knew that the card still sported a credit balance of at least that amount because in our continuing battle for supremacy a few days ago, I had paid all of the previous trip expenses with Old Ron's VISA plus I'd made an extra payment of several thousand dollars. Through the modern miracle of telephone banking, I had made those payments from the old boy's savings account back in Laughlin.

It felt decadently delicious when I informed the miser in one of our shared dreams that his own funds had been used to pay for my lavish driving trip with Sonia. I twisted the knife by gloating that I'd also split our combined wealth into two equal shares and that he could no longer access my half of the funds because they were now protected by my new secret passwords.

Old Ron's apoplectic reaction to my pronouncement was icing on my cake of strategic brilliance.

I grabbed a quick breakfast in the hotel coffee shop before heading to the parking garage.

I had mixed feelings about the driving ordeal which lay ahead of me. In order to rack up maximum distance each day, I'd need to stay on the interstates which tended to be quite tedious.

For once it would have been useful to alternate driving days with the old cheapskate even though that would mean that on my days in reality, I'd wake up in some cheap and dumpy motel.

As I made my way out of the casino to the parking garage, my heart sank as the beautiful sunshine that had greeted me this morning had by now turned into a dark and foreboding rain storm.

I ran across the twenty feet of exposed area from the casino's back door to the covered parking garage entrance while being pelted with rain, and once inside I trudged up the concrete staircase to Level Three.

The sound of intense thunder now filtered in from outside and I had serious misgivings about beginning the trip in such a powerful storm. Drainage in the desert is abominable and deep puddles could easily form on the highway making the drive exceedingly dangerous. Visibility would also be severely restricted.

I spotted my lovely deep burgundy automobile sitting all alone precisely where I had found it last evening.

This section of the third floor in the parking garage appeared almost empty except for my Cadillac. The nearest other vehicle was at least thirty feet away. Since my car was new and unblemished, I wanted to keep it that way and tended to park in the remotest part of these public garages as far away from other cars as possible.

As I approached the Cadillac, I unlocked it and popped open the trunk using the remote buttons on my car key.

When I was still about fifteen feet away from my vehicle, an unbelievable clap of thunder exploded overhead and actually shook the whole parking garage.

I suddenly felt faint and stopped in my tracks, swaying slightly.

My eyes were riveted on my Cadillac when it instantly disappeared at the precise moment that a wave of some unseen force knocked me down.

Disbelief and confusion overwhelmed me as I gingerly stood back up.

My car was gone but a few other cars had miraculously appeared nearby.

I was still a bit woozy. My sports bag had fallen onto the ground beside me when I was knocked down, but the car remote was still firmly grasped in my right hand.

Utterly bewildered by what had just happened, I tried to regroup my muddled thoughts.

Refusing to believe that my car had simply vanished, but also resisting the reasonable conclusion that I had hallucinated, I stood for several minutes trying to piece together an impossible puzzle.

Opting to put some order into this chaos, I rechecked that this was indeed Level Three, Parking Space Seventeen. Then I walked all around this level and through all the other levels in the parking garage. There was no sign of my burgundy Cadillac.

I made my way back to the hotel reception desk where a different clerk was now on duty.

"I just checked out of Room 321 but I'd like to rebook it for tonight. My name's Ronald Smith."

"Certainly sir; I'll just call you up on my screen."

He fiddled with the keyboard for a couple of minutes and looked at me quizzically.

"Are you sure you were in Room 321?"

"Yes."

"Was the room registered under another name?"

"No."

I fumbled around in my pants pocket, extracted the receipt I'd just obtained, and handed it to the clerk.

"The computer gremlins must be mucking up our registration system, sir. I can't find any record of this visit. We show your most recent stay with us as being last September. However, Room 321 is available. How would you like to pay?"

"I'll pay cash. Are you the only desk clerk on duty right now?"

"Yes, Mr. Smith. I've been manning the registration desk alone since my shift began at seven this morning."

Not wanting to appear confused or even demented, I didn't pursue the matter. I thanked the gentleman as he handed me the room key and welcomed me back to the El Cortez.

I'm not a particularly observant guy but I began to notice subtle changes all around me.

The decorations in the lobby seemed more upscale than I had vaguely recalled from earlier this morning. I slowly walked around the casino area attempting to pinpoint other more specific inconsistencies.

One thing did definitely stand out. The cash machine I'd used earlier to extract $3,000 was not in the same location. As an experiment I attempted to withdraw another hundred bucks but the machine rejected my VISA card as being invalid.

Something major was certainly amiss.

When I had checked into this hotel with Sonia before my helicopter injury, a white-haired lady named Celeste who worked in the cashier cage had called out to me and pointed out that she still had Old Ron's joke business card pinned to her desk. Sonia had saved me from embarrassment by jumping in and asking Celeste who she was and how she knew me. Celeste had answered that I'd been a regular guest for the past several years.

I walked by the cashiers' area and spotted Old Ron's friend working at her desk.

"Hello, Celeste," I called through the bars near where she was working.

She turned toward me and her face lit up with recognition.

"Ronald, how nice it is to see you again! It's been many months since you last honored us with your presence. Look, I still have your card. It gives me a chuckle every time I see it. How long are you in town for this visit?"

"I'm only here for a night or two, but I wanted to say hello now in case you're not on duty again before I head back to Canada. It's always comforting to see a friendly familiar face when I'm so far from home."

"Thank you, Ronald. I hope you have a lovely and lucky stay with us. I'm so pleased that you took the time to stop by and say hi."

I didn't know what to make of this development. I knew from Old Ron's diaries that he hadn't been to Las Vegas since September, and that seemed to correspond with the hotel records and Celeste's statement. Somehow my recent existence had now been obliterated along with my Cadillac and my credit card. Celeste had seen me several times over the past couple of weeks but appeared to have no recollection of our recent meetings.

I took the small stairway in the old three-storey section of the El Cortez and entered Room 321.

The layout was identical to what I'd left a couple of hours earlier but the sofa and matching chairs were now black and shiny rather than the faded orange furniture in the room this morning. The drapes and other furniture appeared to be the same but the room had already been cleaned, unusual for this hotel. The maids normally hadn't shown up to clean the room until sometime in the afternoon.

It was time to do some further investigating. I looked out the window. The storm was over and although the sky was still cloudy, the rain had stopped and the sun was persistently attempting to break through the clouds.

I examined the contents of my sports bag. Everything was precisely as I had packed. I opened my wallet and verified that all the cash I'd obtained from the bank machine before I entered the parking garage was still with me. I carefully counted the money while a nagging worry began to plague me that perhaps my entire net worth had been instantly reduced to less than six thousand bucks.

How depressing if Old Ron's wealth was no longer accessible and I was reduced to counting pennies to survive. I wasn't sure if I was even capable of budgeting.

I left the hotel and walked around the Fremont Street Experience which was a couple of blocks away.

While purchasing a phone card, I asked the clerk at ABC Stores where I could find an internet café.

CHAPTER 4 (Where Exactly Am I?)

I located the cozy little restaurant with computers on some of the tables and ordered a hamburger and fries for lunch. I paid for an hour of internet access and sat at one of the computers.

My first project was a failure. I tried to email Sonia's BlackBerry but the computer kept telling me that the message was undeliverable.

Then I accessed the Laughlin Tribune newspaper in Canada. I located the article about Old Ron's mugging on March 23rd. The story appeared identical to the one I'd read after I walked out of the Laughlin Hospital. The piece still contained numerous false assumptions and outright lies. I had contacted the newspaper and the police department as soon as I'd read the putrid piece of garbage and threatened to sue them for defamation. That tactic had resulted in a quick lawsuit settlement of $490,000 and with some of that money I had purchased the Cadillac.

Now, however there were two later mentions of Ronald Smith. The first one was in the April 14th edition and stated that Old Ron was still in a coma in Laughlin General Hospital and that his robbery and mugging remained unsolved. The piece quoted Detective Peter McCabe assuring the public that the police were actively pursuing the matter but that no arrests had yet been made.

Yesterday's edition of the newspaper contained a brief but similar follow-up mentioning that Ronald Smith was still in a coma. It added that the doctors held out little hope for his recovery. A hospital spokeswoman lamented that no relatives had yet come forward but that serious health-care decisions needed to be made in the very near future.

This was incredibly strange.

Sonia and I had been happily motoring around America on April 14th and I had definitely been right here in Las Vegas yesterday.

It was most perplexing.

My lunch came and that distracted me for fifteen minutes.

When my stomach was happy, I searched my Belleville, Ontario hometown newspaper and confirmed that Ronald Smith had been an attorney there for thirty-six years until his retirement in 2012. His retirement picture verified that it was indeed Old Ron.

It appeared that both Old Ron and I now existed at the same time. How was that even possible?

I certainly felt real. Celeste had seen me today and recognized me. Surely I couldn't be some apparition moving around like Bruce Willis in the movie Sixth Sense but not really existing.

It was time to take my investigation to a more direct level.

I left the restaurant and found a quiet bank of pay phones in a nearby casino.

My first call was to Sonia but an automated voice informed me that the number was not in service.

Next I called her parents. After three rings, someone picked up.

"Hello, may I speak with Bernice please?"

"This is Bernice."

"It's Ron Smith calling, Bernice. I've been unable to reach Sonia and wanted to find out how Cecil is faring. Is he recovering from his stroke?"

"I don't understand what you're asking. I'm sorry but what did you say your name was?"

"It's Ron Smith from Canada, Sonia's boyfriend. Is she with you by any chance? I've had bizarre and unexpected delays and haven't even been able to leave Las Vegas for Chicago yet. Sonia probably thinks I'll be arriving there tomorrow."

An eerie silence ensued, followed by Bernice stammering, "I don't think I understand you correctly. My granddaughter Karen is here. I'll let you speak with her."

Karen came on the line and I repeated what I'd just told Bernice.

"Are you sure you have the right number?" she queried in a cold tone of voice.

"Of course I'm sure, Karen. You're married to Jeff Chandler and have a sister, Nancy. You called Sonia on Tuesday on her BlackBerry while we were vacationing in Las Vegas and told her about Cecil's stroke. Sonia flew back to Chicago that same evening and I expected to drive there beginning on Wednesday morning but now it's Friday and I haven't even left. By any chance is Sonia there with you? I really need to speak with her."

There was no response other than dead air for at least a minute, at which time an aggressive male voice announced that it was Dr. Jeffrey Chandler who demanded that I repeat what I'd just told Karen.

Despite my utter confusion about this bizarre reaction to my phone call, I complied. When I had finished, I pleaded with Jeff, "Will somebody please tell me where Sonia is and what's going on?"

Jeff responded in a crisp professional manner that oozed skepticism.

"Have you actually met any members of our family, Ron?"

"Of course I have. Surely you remember me?"

"I most certainly do not. When did we meet? Please be as specific as possible."

I had no idea what to think about this eerie turn of events, but nevertheless I tried to explain.

"Well, I first met Sonia at the Rushmore Arms on April 1st when she was dining with her friends Connie and Darlene. Sonia and I hit it off and she gave me a tour of Chicago the next day and invited me to her sixtieth birthday party at your house that evening. That's where I met the whole family including Cecil and Bernice, you and Karen, Nancy and her husband as well as Allan Cranbull, Sonia's ex-spouse. Sonia and I spent the next few days together and then she agreed to accompany me on my driving trip. We were having a tremendous holiday until Sonia got Karen's phone call about Cecil's stroke and had to fly back to Chicago."

Jeff interjected at that point.

"Did I understand you correctly that you were at Sonia's sixtieth birthday party at my home just last month?"

"Yes; surely you haven't forgotten."

"My memory isn't perfect. Did we meet anywhere else?"

"Yes, Jeff; we later met at Sonia's condominium a couple of days before we left on the driving trip. We had you, Karen, Bernice and Cecil over for supper so that we could get the family's blessing about taking the holiday together despite my rather unique impediment."

"And what might that be?" Jeff asked in a dubious voice.

"I was mugged in Canada in March and woke up from a coma a few days later with no memory of my past life. I had you talk with Dr. Long in Laughlin about my amnesia and both you and Karen were satisfied that I posed no threat to Sonia. Why do I get the distinct impression that you haven't got a clue about any of this?"

"I can't decide whether this is a sick joke or some type of scam. Perhaps you're just troubled, but whatever you're up to, I'm warning you. Don't call here again or we'll be forced to bring in the police."

I was awash in confusion.

"Wait, Jeff, don't hang up yet. Will you please let me speak directly with Sonia? Surely I don't sound like a fraud or a crazy person. I'm just as confused as you are about why no one in your family remembers me."

My tone must have conveyed sincerity because Jeff's tone softened a bit.

"Had you ever met Sonia before April 1st, Ron?"

"No."

"You didn't attend school with her, did you?"

"No, I'm from Canada and met Sonia at the Rushmore Arms in the Indian Restaurant like I said."

"Where's the Rushmore Arms?"

"It's on Lakeshore Drive near downtown."

I heard Jeff yell for Karen to bring him the Chicago phone book. The sound of rustling papers followed.

"There's no such hotel listed in the phone directory, Ron. How do you explain that?"

"I'm absolutely mystified. This has been the strangest day imaginable."

"Why do you say that?"

"This morning when I went to get my Cadillac and start out for Chicago, the entire car disappeared right before my eyes. It vanished just like magic and all I was left with was the car key remote. Then I began noticing subtle changes everywhere, like the color of the furniture in my hotel room. The clerk had no record of my having just checked out of the hotel even though I still had the receipt in my pocket. A casino cashier who had spoken with Sonia and me two weeks earlier no longer remembered and said that she hadn't seen me since last year. Now Sonia's family has no recollection of me and I discovered this morning on the internet that I'm supposed to be languishing in a coma back in Canada even though I'm here in Las Vegas."

"Ron, I'm so sorry for your confusion, but I can't make sense of anything you said. Sonia died last December in a vicious mugging here in Chicago. The stress caused Cecil to have a serious stroke two months after that and he passed away in March. It's very worrisome that you seem to know so much about the identity of our family. I strongly recommend that you see a therapist about your delusions. I don't mean to be harsh, but please don't call here again. Your gibberish will only upset Bernice and she's got enough troubles filling her plate as it is. Will you promise not to contact any of us again?"

I hesitated a moment, totally demoralized and confused, but then I told Jeff that I'd respect his wishes. I even thanked him for being so kind and understanding.

30

When I had finished the call, the import of Jeff's revelations finally sunk in.

My beloved Sonia didn't even exist in this world and my ramblings made me seem insane.

I was heartbroken.

I wandered around the downtown area in a daze trying to collect my thoughts.

It was blatantly obvious that the truth from my perspective was unpalatable to anyone else.

If I wanted to survive here, wherever "here" was, I had to abruptly change my tactics.

Somehow neither I as New Ron nor Sonia existed in this particular world. The thought of a life without Sonia was too depressing to envisage.

I returned to the bank of pay phones and called the Laughlin, Ontario Police Department where I was put through to Detective Peter McCabe.

"Hello, sir, my name is Donald Smith and I'm the twin brother of Ronald Smith. I just read on the internet that Ron was robbed and mugged and is still in the hospital."

"Thank you so much for calling, Mr. Smith. Yes, I'm sorry to say, the prognosis isn't very promising for your brother. Where are you phoning from?"

"I'm in Las Vegas."

"Is there any possibility that you can come up here to Canada and look after your brother's affairs?"

"I'll try to book a flight in the next day or so, and I'll call you once I arrive. Is Ron still unconscious?"

"He is, as far as I know. The hospital has promised to call me if he revives. His

31

attackers are still at large. How were you able to find out about your brother?"

I thought for a moment and then decided to travel down Eerie Lane again.

"Ron and I are identical twins and we shared a dream last night. He told me about being mugged in Laughlin and said that the men who robbed him were Bobby Lisowski and Darrel. They divulged their names in the course of the robbery and were trying to come up with three hundred bucks in order to make a drug purchase from someone named Bucky. Ron said that the men stole $80 in cash and his University of Waterloo Alumni watch. The dream was so vivid and detailed that when I woke up this morning, I decided to check the internet. Lo and behold, I quickly found the newspaper articles and discovered that you were the investigating detective."

"That's about the most unorthodox lead I've ever had, but I'll check it out for you. I suppose stranger things have happened. I look forward to meeting you when you get here, Mr. Smith. Perhaps I'll even have some good news about the crime."

I immediately walked back to the internet café to check out air fares. The best bet was a United Airlines flight to Detroit leaving tomorrow morning but I encountered a glitch. With no useable credit card, I couldn't book it.

While I was on the computer, I tried to find the Rushmore Arms in Chicago but, just as Jeff had indicated, it didn't exist.

I walked back to the pay phones and called the airline directly only to discover that it had a tiny sub-office in the Golden Jackpot Casino downtown. I whipped over there and was able to purchase with cash a ticket for

32

tomorrow's flight. It irritated me that I was thrilled that the ticket cost only $167 including taxes. Surely I wasn't morphing into Old Ron the cheapskate.

I was somewhat consoled when I reminded myself that I really was on a strict budget at the moment. Paying a reasonable price for something didn't automatically turn me into some kind of financial freak like my disgusting alter ego. Until I ascertained whether any of Old Ron's money was accessible to me, I needed to conserve my funds.

I purchased a six-pack of premium beer and walked back to the El Cortez where I scoured the parking garage and confirmed that my Cadillac had not miraculously reappeared.

I ate supper at the hotel coffee shop and booked the hotel's complimentary early morning shuttle to the Las Vegas airport.

Over the next few hours I drank beer and tried to comprehend what was happening to me. I had only limited success.

There was no doubt that I was totally real but stuck in this strange alternate world. Somehow in that thunderstorm I had become separated from both my Cadillac and Sonia's reality.

This was extreme science fiction but I was now living it and could no longer deny that I'd been transported into a different realm.

By the fourth beer I realized that more surprises would likely be forthcoming. How could Old Ron and I both continue to exist in the same world?

I ordered a wake-up call for six in the morning and crawled into bed at ten o'clock, wondering if Old Ron and I would soon be sharing another dream.

CHAPTER 5 (Withered Old Ron)

I awoke with a start when the phone rang
with my wake-up call.

For a moment I lay on the bed trying to
recollect whether I'd had any dreams but
concluded that I had not. My watch showed that
it was Saturday so I hadn't missed a day. This
was my third day in a row without the
unwelcome intrusion of Old Ron interrupting my
existence. That was the only positive aspect
of my current dilemma.

The couch and chair in the room were shiny
black and new, not old and faded orange. That
indicated that I was still in this alternate
world where Sonia had been murdered and Old
Ron was still in the Laughlin General
Hospital.

I quickly showered and did a speedy run
through the parking garage to ensure that my
Cadillac was still missing. It was depressing
to think that the beauty had cost me $59,000
but I'd only enjoyed its luxury for six weeks.

I wondered if I still existed in the other
world and was continuing to enjoy my upscale
wheels on route to meet up with my true love
in Chicago. I was also curious as to whether
my dream battle with Old Ron had been
successful in expunging the cheapskate from
existence in that realm. If so, then Sonia and
I would have a marvelous future together. It
was too bad that I was no longer around in
that world to appreciate it. I longed
desperately to be transported back to that
world but a gnawing in the pit of my gut made
me believe that both Old Ron and I no longer
existed in that realm. Poor Sonia would have

34

no idea what had happened to the cheapskate or to me. My true love would be frantic with worry.

I still had time for a quick breakfast in the casino coffee shop before heading to the front hotel entrance to catch the shuttle bus to the airport.

A pleasant surprise awaited me a few minutes later. The free shuttle turned out to be a shiny black limousine with a pretty young girl at the wheel, and I was the sole passenger.

That small taste of my former lavish lifestyle was most welcome to take my mind off the chaos now permeating my life.

As I sat in the back seat and glanced around, my eye was caught by a brochure showing my driver topless and touting nude limo rides. It was apparent that in this alternate universe, folks in Las Vegas still did just about anything to make a buck.

I had no difficulty checking in and obtaining my boarding pass. Fortunately Old Ron's Ontario Driver's License had been in my wallet and his Canadian Passport had been in my pants pocket at the moment I was transported to this world.

I'd been a bit concerned that those pieces of identification from the other realm might not pass scrutiny here and would wind up being as useless as my credit card.

The flight departure was only delayed a few minutes. Three hours later I was in the Detroit airport seeking directions to the bus station. Luckily there was a regular shuttle bus that stopped there so I waited patiently for the next bus at five o'clock Detroit time.

The logistics of getting from Detroit to Laughlin were somewhat complicated and entailed a short ride to Windsor. Old Ron's passport worked like a charm in getting me accepted at the Canadian border.

At the Windsor bus station, I caught another bus to my final destination and arrived at the downtown Laughlin bus terminal at quarter to ten in the evening.

I walked the quarter mile to Old Ron's apartment rather than waste a few bucks on a taxi.

Not completely certain whether Old Ron's living arrangements in this world were identical to what I'd seen in the other reality, I thought it prudent to knock on old Mrs. Cotter's door since I wasn't supposed to have a key.

When she opened her apartment door, I thought her eyes were going to pop out of her head.

"Ron, you're okay," she blurted out. "Thank God. We were so worried that you weren't going to make it."

"Actually ma'am, I'm Ron's twin brother, Don. I just found out about Ron's accident yesterday and flew to Laughlin as soon as I could. I've been in touch with Detective McCabe and will meet with him tomorrow. I'd like to stay in Ron's apartment while I'm here because I've got to try and get his affairs in order."

"Of course you can stay there, Don. I'm Liz Cotter and I'm so thankful that you've arrived. I didn't know what to do. Ron's rent isn't paid and his mail is piling up. I took the liberty of entering his unit and discarding any food that might spoil. Let me get you a key and I'll come upstairs with you."

As we walked up the stairs to the top or third floor, I asked Mrs. Cotter how much the rent was, and she confirmed that it was $500 a month. She mentioned that Ron had already prepaid the April rent before he was attacked. I assured her that I'd convert some of my US money into Canadian on Monday morning and pay Ron's May rent. I saw extreme relief in Mrs. Cotter's eyes. I realized how precarious her financial situation was from my short time living here, albeit in the other world, for almost a full week after I emerged from the coma.

Mrs. Cotter showed me all the mail that had piled up on Old Ron's desk, and quipped that perusing it would certainly keep me busy for a while.

"I'm so sorry Don, but I haven't been over to visit Ron for about three weeks. It's too far to walk and no one has offered me a ride lately. Ron's car is sitting in the parking area but I didn't want to use it without permission. Ron never even mentioned that he had a twin brother. You can't imagine how surprised I was to see you at my door."

"I've been away from Canada for a long time and didn't even know that Ron had moved to Laughlin. I haven't spoken with him since shortly after his wife died in 2005. I'll head over to the hospital first thing tomorrow. Thanks for the key, and I'll keep you posted as fully as I can. I'll also make satisfactory arrangements regarding future rent payments."

I said goodnight and looked around the downscale apartment whose twin had been my temporary home. Strangely, everything appeared perfectly identical to how I remembered it. So far this reality in Laughlin was precisely the same as the one I woke up in. I wondered why the Las Vegas and Chicago in this reality were both somewhat different from the other world.

Despite the long day of travel, I was still on Las Vegas time so I sat at Old Ron's black wooden desk with the fake white marble top and began to go through his personal effects, exactly as I had done in the other world right after I'd escaped from the Laughlin hospital.

It took a while to open his mail but that allowed me to peruse his latest investment statements. Old Ron was remarkably organized. All his other bills were paid either by automatic debit or had been prepaid well in advance. Even his completed 2014 income tax return had been sent in before he was mugged.

In Sonia's world I had enraged Old Ron by splitting our combined assets down the middle in such a way that he couldn't access the portion I considered to belong to me. In this new world Old Ron appeared to have the same investments and net worth as before. His signature was still identical to mine, so I signed his name on several blank checks in order to facilitate my ability to deal with matters.

It was patently obvious that I had not existed in this world because there was no record of any lawsuit against the newspaper or the cops.

Eventually fatigue crept up on me and I hit the sack well after midnight.

...

I didn't wake up until after nine o'clock. It had been another dreamless sleep.

I phoned the hospital to check with administration and they were so grateful to hear from me that, despite it being Sunday, they made an appointment for a woman to meet me there at one o'clock to discuss pressing care matters.

Then I called the police department and left a message for Detective Peter McCabe advising him that I was meeting Ms. Deborah Bronson in Ron's room at the hospital at one o'clock in case he wanted to meet me there.

There was nothing much to eat in the refrigerator which was almost empty, and the cupboards were almost completely bare. I drank a can of Pepsi since there was no milk, tea or coffee.

I got on Old Ron's computer, which was not password protected, and scanned the newspapers for Belleville, Laughlin and Toronto.

From what I searched, there didn't appear to be any changes between this world and the other one until the period at which I popped out of the coma in the other universe.

I found Old Ron's car keys for his depressingly low-end 2002 Chevrolet Cavalier and decided to drive around Laughlin in search of discrepancies.

The little beast started right up and I took a brief tour of the portion of Laughlin I'd explored in the other world.

The decrepit Kaufmann Arms looked identical to how I remembered it. I debated whether to have breakfast there but couldn't bring myself to eat in the loathsome dump.

I found a decent restaurant and treated myself to a hearty steak and eggs late breakfast.

I continued driving around but nothing struck me as changed in any way. In Chicago the Rushmore Arms didn't exist in this world, and I'd noticed numerous changes at the El Cortez in Las Vegas.

It was eerie pretending to be someone in this world who didn't exist.

I pulled into the Laughlin General Hospital parking lot shortly after noon and found Old Ron close to death in a ward with two other near-death patients. I was a bit leery about touching him in case that triggered some extreme cosmic reaction, but I relented after a few minutes and held Old Ron's hand.

A few minutes later Detective McCabe entered the room. I pretended that I didn't know him as we introduced ourselves.

"Your dream tip paid off in spades," he grinned. "Not only did I locate the fellows who robbed your brother, but they were so flustered when I showed up at their door that they proceeded to confess to a whole string of crimes over the past couple of years. Your brother's watch was found at their apartment but it has to be held for now as evidence. Do you think he'll ever get to wear it again?"

"I don't know. I haven't talked to a doctor yet. Ron won't even be sixty-five until July 26th, but he looks about a hundred years old in this bed. It's extremely upsetting. You're welcome to sit in on my meeting with Ms. Bronson if you'd like."

"Thank you for that, Don. I should try to obtain a current prognosis regarding your brother before deciding what charges the muggers should face."

I felt a vague uneasiness about Old Ron's critical condition. If this near-corpse in the hospital bed passed away, would I expire simultaneously? I was definitely in uncharted territory.

My best guess and fervent hope was that somehow I was now a completely different entity from this decaying version of Old Ron. I certainly felt perfectly healthy.

Ms. Bronson arrived and led McCabe and I to a meeting room where a hospital administrator named Michael Black was waiting for us. Bronson paged Dr. Karen Schmidt who showed up within two minutes to provide me with a summary of Old Ron's condition.

"I'm sorry to say that we hold out no hope whatsoever that your brother is going to regain consciousness. Too much time has elapsed. A panel of three physicians including myself has recommended that Mr. Smith be taken off life support. Please accept our sincere condolences, sir. Do you have any medical questions?"

"I don't, doctor. Thank you for being so candid."

Detective McCabe interjected at that point. He turned to me and asked, "Given what Dr. Schmidt has just said, do you have any input into what level of criminal charges the two muggers should face?"

I thought about what Old Ron had told me about the incident in our shared dreams. The two thugs were complete idiots.

"Use your discretion, Detective. Anything you decide is acceptable to me. At least you've arrested them and they've confessed to assaulting Ron and various other crimes. It appears that justice has finally prevailed."

McCabe thanked me and left the meeting.

The doctor took that opportunity to leave as well.

Ms. Bronson then took control.

"Do you have any power of attorney for your brother?"

"No, in fact I haven't even spoken with him since 2005 after his wife died of cancer. I did find his Ontario Health Card in his apartment and brought it with me. Do you need it?"

"That's a huge help, sir. We hadn't been able to locate his health records using just his name and address. Does he have any other relatives besides you?"

"We have no one but each other. Neither of us ever had children or other siblings and our parents are long ago deceased."

"Do you know if your brother has a Last Will and Testament?"

"I haven't found anything in his apartment but I'll take a closer look. Since he's a retired lawyer, I'd be surprised if he doesn't have one."

"Has your brother made any prepaid funeral arrangements?"

"I don't know but I'll try to find out. No disrespect intended, but Ron was a cheap bastard, so I doubt very much if he's already paid for his own funeral."

"Do you know whether he has any private medical insurance?"

"Again, I'll look though his papers and bill payment records, but so far I've found no insurance documents. Does he owe any money to the hospital?"

"Now that we have Mr. Smith's Ontario Health Card details, I'll verify tomorrow that the card is valid in which case everything should be covered. Would you be willing to sign a consent form on the patient's behalf authorizing life support to be terminated?"

When I answered in the affirmative, Mr. Black advised that he'd have the necessary paperwork available tomorrow and we set up another meeting for Tuesday morning. He recommended that I make preliminary arrangements with a funeral home to have Old Ron's body transferred from the hospital after he passes away.

CHAPTER 6 (Robbing Myself)

I dropped in to see Mrs. Cotter before
going up to the apartment and told her the sad
news. I asked the lady to tell me what Ron had
been up to since he arrived in Laughlin.

Her reply seemed identical to what I'd
learned in the other world. Old Ron had
rescued Tammy Mick, a runaway he found when he
first stayed at the Kaufmann Arms. Tammy had
been with Ron when he first looked at Mrs.
Cotter's vacant apartment on the top floor,
and last night I had noticed that Tammy's
graduation picture hung in the apartment just
like it had in the other realm.

In this reality Old Ron had also set up
Tiffany and Amelia with the Wilson brothers
with spectacular results, and Ron had driven
Mrs. Cotter to get groceries until the violent
mugging sent him on his unplanned hospital
visit.

Back in the apartment, I located and
carefully examined Old Ron's daily journal
which was stored on his computer. It was a
carbon copy of what I recalled from the other
world.

This world was remarkably similar to the
other one as far as Old Ron and Laughlin were
concerned. I wondered what had triggered Sonia
and Cecil's deaths in this world along with
the disappearance of the Rushmore Arms in
Chicago and the new furniture in the El Cortez
Hotel Casino in Las Vegas. Except for those
few differences, and now my separate
existence, everything else I'd encountered in
the two worlds seemed to mirror each other.

I found Old Ron's Last Will and Testament
in an envelope at the back of the bottom desk
drawer in a hidden compartment, but it was
useless. He had prepared it just after he
married Hannah and she was the sole
beneficiary and executor. There was no
residual clause dealing with his estate in the
event that Hannah predeceased him.

Old Ron had inserted a recent note in the
envelope reminding himself to contact a lawyer
in order to draft a new Will. Under the note
he had jotted down a list of things to
consider and listed "Pet charities, needy
friends here in Laughlin, Belleville and
Laughlin libraries," and Old Ron had inserted
a question mark after each item on the list.

From that discovery I assumed that Old Ron
hadn't yet decided on any specific
beneficiaries. I found no power of attorney
and assumed that, being all alone, Old Ron
trusted so one sufficiently to give anyone
control over his affairs.

I began to think of my own self-
preservation.

Once Old Ron died, I'd be penniless except
for the money in my wallet. I couldn't write a
check to Donald Smith because I had no
identification in that assumed name so
wouldn't be able to cash a check.

Luckily the little hermit had listed all
his passwords and pin numbers in an envelope
containing his bank cards and he had also
noted the maximum daily cash withdrawals
permitted on each account.

Hoping that Sunday was considered to be a
separate banking day for account withdrawal
purposes, I drove to both of Old Ron's banks
and withdrew the maximum permitted from the

ATM's. That netted me $2,000 and I resolved to
hit the banks every day until Old Ron died.

I paid the May apartment rent to Mrs.
Cotter using some of that cash.

On Monday morning after another dreamless
night, I was fairly confident that there would
be no more alternating of appearances. It
seemed that I was a completely separate Ronald
Smith in this parallel world.

I phoned Ben Van Huizen, the lawyer who
owned the building in Belleville where Old Ron
had rented his apartment as well as his legal
office until he retired. Ben was forwarding to
Laughlin whatever bit of straggling mail
continued to be sent to the old Belleville
address.

He was very concerned when I told him what
had happened to Ron, and he was a fountain of
useful information about the cheapskate's
affairs. Ben had never done any legal work for
Old Ron but seemed to know him very well.

"I'm certain that your brother never made
any personal funeral arrangements. When Hannah
passed away, Ron selected the most basic of
cremation services and buried her ashes in
Hannah's late parents' plot. I remember how
annoyed he was at the newspaper over the cost
of the obituary notice and at the cemetery for
the small fee they charged to add Hannah's
name and details onto her parents' headstone.
I guess I don't have to tell you how frugal
Ron is. He was also very private and in fact
never even mentioned that he had a twin
brother."

"We're identical twins," I answered, "but
we weren't raised together. I was sent off as
a very young baby to live in South America."

I didn't offer any additional information,
realizing that blatant lies shouldn't be too

46

specific. I thanked Ben for the information and told him that I'd keep him posted as to Ron's progress.

I called Mr. Black at the Laughlin hospital and provided him with the information I'd gleaned about Ron's lack of additional health insurance or any power of attorney. We confirmed our meeting tomorrow to settle Ron's medical and hospital affairs.

I hit Old Ron's banks and snatched another thousand bucks from each bank machine.

I grabbed supper at a fast food joint. Since there was beer in Old Ron's fridge, I cracked open a brew and mulled over my own future.

Since I wasn't supposed to exist in this world, I concluded that it would be prudent to live a quiet life far away from Laughlin and Belleville.

I toyed with the idea of going to Chicago. It struck me that Sonia might hold the key to a fuller understanding of why the two worlds had branched off in slightly different directions. Perhaps I'd be able to investigate why the Rushmore Arms didn't exist in this reality. At least Chicago seemed to be a logical place to start my quest for answers.

Residing in the USA permanently after Old Ron passed away also held some attraction. I'd be far from prying Canadian authorities and my disappearance after Old Ron's death would lead to a boatload of questions, especially after it was discovered that he never had a twin brother. If I remained in Canada, at some point my lack of any ID would inevitably lead to unanswerable queries.

The only concrete plan of action I resolved was that tomorrow I'd change most of my Canadian cash into American funds.

I fell asleep pondering this surprising existence of two alternate realities.

Why was Sonia alive and loved in my previous world but dead and gone in this one?

When I awoke on Tuesday morning, I finally had vivid recollections of a dream. Sonia and I were in San Antonio on a small tour boat drifting blissfully on the Riverwalk canal system, hand in hand and excitedly talking about what a lovely city we were seeing and how wonderful it was to have found each other.

That was the first dream in my short period of existence that dealt with my life as New Ron. Excluding the shared dreams with Old Ron, I'd only experienced two previous dreams, both of which encompassed real events in Old Ron's past. One of those dreams related to a slot jackpot Old Ron had hit at the El Cortez years earlier, and the other was about a church service he had attended near that casino. Old Ron had confirmed in a shared dream that both events actually happened on September 19th, 1999 while he was in Las Vegas on a vacation with Hannah.

I attended at Laughlin General Hospital and signed all the forms required to pull the plug on Old Ron and transfer his body to a local funeral home.

Dr. Schmidt and Michael Black joined me in Old Ron's hospital room where the doctor oversaw the unhooking of my counterpart from all his tubes and monitors.

The doctor advised that it would likely take two or three days for Ron's systems to completely shut down.

After they left, I sat with him for an hour, holding his hand and silently communicating that I fervently hoped that he approved of what I had just authorized.

I realized that I was beginning to view Old Ron as my actual brother rather than the opposite side of my own persona.

On the way home I stopped at both banks and decided to be more brazen.

Hoping that no one serving me would be aware that their real customer lay dying in the hospital, I purchased $4,000 of US cash at each bank, paying for same out of Old Ron's accounts. As I completed each transaction I grew more daring and ordered an additional $5,000 in American cash at each bank to be picked up tomorrow and again signed for the withdrawal from Old Ron's savings accounts.

On the way out of each branch I also withdrew the maximum from their bank machines. My "great escape" war chest was rapidly growing.

Back in the apartment, after picking up a submarine sandwich and potato chips for supper, I drank beer and wrote out a holograph Will for Old Ron. Writing out the terms by hand overcame the legal requirement of witnesses.

I duly revoked any prior Wills and appointed Elizabeth Cotter and Carl Kaufmann as the Estate Trustees. I specifically stated that I was making this holograph Will to ensure that my affairs would be in order in the event that I passed away before I could contact a lawyer, and I chastised myself in the document for not making a new Will shortly after Hannah died.

I made bequests of $100,000 to Tammy Mick, Amelia Cole and Tiffany Wright, the three young girls Old Ron had met and assisted during his time in Laughlin.

Gifts of $75,000 were made to the Corby Public Library in Belleville, the Laughlin

49

Public Library, the Belleville Humane Society and the Laughlin Humane Society.

The car, furniture and all personal effects were bequeathed to Elizabeth Cotter, and finally the residue of the estate was divided 30 percent to Elizabeth Cotter and 70 percent to Carl Kaufmann.

I duly signed Old Ron's name and dated the document March 16th, 2015 being a week before he got mugged.

To make it appear even more legitimate, I wrote "Cancelled by Ronald Smith on March 16th, 2015" on Old Ron's previous Will and signed his name. I also left Old Ron's note reminding himself to update his Will.

A part of me was heartsick to see what felt like my own assets being distributed to others when I had a desperate need for money of my own. I couldn't name myself as a beneficiary because proper identification would be an absolute requirement before I could collect any inheritance, and all that would accomplish would be to land me in complicated legal trouble.

Somewhat satisfied that I had settled Old Ron's affairs in this world as closely as I guessed his wishes would have been, I got the brilliant idea of using Old Ron's computer to search the internet for more information on the Poniecki family in the Chicago of this world.

Eventually I found the obituaries for both Cecil and Sonia.

Cecil Poniecki died on March 30th, 2015. The death notice stated that he had been predeceased by his beloved daughter, Sonia. The remainder of the information in the obituary corresponded to the family I had met in the other realm.

Sonia's death notice had the sad words, "Suddenly and tragically on December 12th, 2014 beloved mother, grandmother and daughter Sonia Poniecki was taken home to God."

Neither date of death had any significance that I could decipher.

For the next couple of hours I searched Sonia's names in all the Chicago newspapers, both her previous married name and the maiden name I knew her by. Nothing came up under "Cranbull" but under "Poniecki" there were several hits relating to her murder.

Sonia was savagely beaten to death in the parking lot of her condominium building and, according to the newspapers, the police had found no witnesses and no clues whatsoever. Her purse wasn't taken nor the money in it, and there was no evidence of sexual assault. Sonia's ex-husband had been out of town on a business trip and no suspects were ever named in the press. One very brief follow-up piece appeared in one paper a few days after Cecil's obituary, and it stated that the police had tentatively concluded that Sonia's murder must have been simply a random act of violence. Although the police continued their investigation, the article gave the distinct impression that solving the crime was highly unlikely.

By the time I'd knocked back my fourth beer, fatigue suddenly overtook me. I turned off the computer and got into bed.

What an upsetting day it had been!

It was difficult enough unplugging Old Ron and giving away his and my entire fortune, but reading about Sonia's murder was indescribably depressing.

CHAPTER 7 (More Shared Dreams)

The next thing I knew I was on a cloud again, just like I had been with Old Ron, except this time I was alone.

I glanced around and realized that I was back in Room 321 at the El Cortez Hotel and Casino in Las Vegas.

How strange!

I wondered if Old Ron would be making an appearance in this dream.

It dawned on me that the sofa and matching chairs were black and new rather than orange and worn, which indicated that this dream was taking place in the world in which Sonia was dead and in which both Old Ron and I now co-existed as separate entities.

A crackling or sizzling sound began and a small cloud began forming about eight feet away on the opposite side of the hotel room. This was the same scenario that had arisen in each of my previous shared dreams with Old Ron.

I sincerely hoped that the cheapskate wasn't going to give me a hard time for forging his Will and absconding with some of his cash. I braced myself for a confrontation.

To my great surprise it was Cecil Poniecki who slowly materialized, and he appeared overwhelmed and in utter confusion.

"Welcome to my dream, Cecil. It's good to see you again."

He stared at me speechlessly with absolutely no hint of recognition.

"Am I being taken to Heaven?" he finally stammered.

"Not tonight, Cecil. This dream is taking place in Las Vegas. Don't you recognize me?"

"No, I'm so sorry, but I don't know who you are."

"It's Ron Smith from Canada, Sonia's boyfriend."

"My daughter was murdered," he answered harshly. "Sonia never dated a Canadian. How do you know our names?"

"I think I'm beginning to see the broader picture, Cecil."

I then proceeded to explain briefly the existence of two separate worlds, and outlined what had happened to me since my Cadillac vanished.

When I'd finished, Cecil asked me to tell him about my life with Sonia in the other world. I complied and stressed how much in love we had been and what strange complications had arisen when Old Ron joined the party. Cecil was mystified when I mentioned my shared dreams with my alter ego.

"Some things are just possibly beginning to make a bit of sense," Cecil responded. "Am I still alive in that alternate world?"

"You were as of a week ago, but that's the last contact I've had with Sonia since she went through security at the Las Vegas airport just prior to her flight to Chicago. If you died in your world on March 30th, where have you been since then?"

"I'm not sure, but it might have been some type of limbo. I've been able to observe things and eavesdrop on the creatures, but they don't seem to be aware of my presence. I had no idea why I was conscious or where I was. You're the first person I've been able to communicate with."

"What creatures are you talking about?"

"There are just two of them, shapeless apparitions, and they've become extremely agitated. From what I can gather, something has gone horribly wrong with some experiment or contest they're having. I haven't been able to make any sense of their situation, but they definitely spoke of illogical differences between their two toys. Perhaps the information you just provided will make it easier for me to understand things. You have no idea how contented it makes me to know that Sonia has found happiness in that other realm."

The crackling sound started up again and Cecil began to vaporize. All I had time to say was that I hoped we'd meet again.

When I woke up in the morning, the dream was crystal clear in my mind, but now there were far more questions than answers. I simply didn't have enough data with which to draw any rational conclusions.

After breakfast I dropped back to the two banks and picked up the US money I'd ordered yesterday, and was pleased that no one gave the transactions a second glance. The anonymity of modern banking was certainly a boon to fraudsters, not that I considered myself to be a member of that spurious class.

Emboldened by my progress to date, I withdrew $1,000 cash from each banking machine on my way out of the banks.

I spent most of the day sitting with Old Ron and his equally comatose ward mates. Although I couldn't detect any noticeable difference in the old boy, the nurses and doctors who filtered in from time to time told me that it wouldn't be long now before Old Ron passed away peacefully.

Feeling that I should somehow set the stage for Old Ron's death, I dropped into the Kaufmann Arms and shocked Carl when he saw me.

After introducing myself as Ron's twin brother, I disclosed to Carl that I had found my brother's handwritten Will naming Carl co-trustee of the estate along with Mrs. Cotter, and that Carl was also one of the main beneficiaries.

I gave Liz Cotter the same information when I returned to her tenement building.

Both of them were unable to completely mask their mixed emotions, sadness over Ron's tragedy stirred in with excitement about the prospect of an unexpected inheritance.

Since it was only four o'clock, I telephoned Peter Long who was a lawyer and friend of Old Ron, and made an appointment for five o'clock.

I brought along the handwritten Will to leave with Peter for safe-keeping, and advised the attorney that both Carl and Mrs. Cotter had agreed that Peter should handle the legal work for the estate. I also gave Peter a list which I'd printed off Old Ron's computer detailing his investments.

When Peter tactfully mentioned that Ron had never mentioned having a twin brother, I concocted a story about living most of my life in South America. I added that I'd be heading back there in the very near future and that I was wealthy and felt no disappointment about being disinherited.

"Ron and I barely knew each other and last spoke more than ten years ago. We were effective strangers who happened to share the same womb for nine months."

Peter had me sign a Release waiving any possible claim I might have against Ron's estate, and I was happy to do so. Peter examined the Will carefully and concluded that it appeared to be legally valid.

I stressed that my brother detested wasting money, that he was to be cremated immediately following his death, and that there was to be no funeral service or newspaper obituary of any sort.

Since I was already downtown, I ate a fancy supper at the Beaumont Hotel in the same dining-room in which Old Ron's muggers had indulged in a free feast, mostly liquid, immediately after robbing Old Ron and leaving him for dead. I was pleased that the brutes had finally been caught.

Satisfied that I'd tied up a lot of loose ends today, I dropped back to the hospital and sat with Old Ron until visiting hours ended at eight o'clock.

As I climbed under the covers later, I was fervently anticipating another meeting with Cecil in dreamland.

Sure enough, I was soon back on my dream cloud watching Cecil form on his own fluffy seat.

Cecil was extremely agitated and immediately began talking a mile a minute.

"One of those monsters murdered my Sonia. I've been overhearing them ever since I last met you here. One of them selected my beautiful daughter randomly as the sacrificial lamb in some depraved experiment to measure the cumulative effects of the removal of one solitary human being from just one of the worlds. The two creatures observe both worlds but one of them grew bored watching two identical peas in a pod, so it chose to play God and murdered Sonia in order to study the changes her absence would cause."

56

"Did you find out how they did it?" I asked incredulously.

"I think so. From what I think I understand, they're the only two beings in existence in their own tiny realm. One of them has the ability to shape itself into other forms and then propel those forms into its toy, which appears to be the world I lived in. I believe that it inserted itself into my world as a human being for the sole purpose of killing poor Sonia. Then it returned back to the creature it was created from. That might explain why the Chicago police found no clues to work with and the crime went unsolved."

"I've been pondering what you told me in our last dream when you mentioned that the creatures had run into some major problem. Have you any idea what went wrong with their experiment?"

"They haven't figured out yet what's happened, but it appears to involve the extent of the rapidly emerging differences between the two worlds. The creatures believe that those escalating changes are statistically and logically impossible, and they're both frantic about it."

The crackling resumed and Cecil quickly deteriorated before anything else could be said by either of us.

When I awoke, the contents of our shared dream were fully vivid in my mind. The reason for our continued dream meetings totally eluded me since both of us were completely helpless to take any action.

At least some of my questions were being vaguely answered.

CHAPTER 8 (Death of Old Ron)

Thursday was a lovely day, sunny and warm, so I walked to a restaurant near the hospital for breakfast and then continued on to visit Old Ron.

He had deteriorated significantly overnight and I realized that the end was near, so I resolved to stay with him until the end.

I sat at Old Ron's bedside and held the old miser's hand, wishing that we had gotten along more amicably in our shared dreams but realizing how impossible that would have been given our diametrically opposing outlooks on just about everything plus our intense rivalry over Sonia.

It was difficult separating this innocent version of Old Ron from the scoundrel in my other world who had lusted after my true love and baited me about how much Sonia had enjoyed having rampant sex with him.

The concept of two parallel worlds was almost too outrageous to grasp despite the mounting evidence.

There was no response from Old Ron who was really no more than a human vegetable now, and I was certain that he had no inkling that I'd been visiting him every day since arriving in Laughlin. Old Ron would never know that his muggers had been captured and that his accumulated wealth would help several needy friends and worthy organizations. His estate would have been a dreadful mess if I hadn't written out a new Will for him. I hadn't learned much about our family from reading Old Ron's journal, but I suspected that his closest living relatives were probably second or third cousins. At least my forgery pushed Old Ron's money into the hands of organizations and people he knew and admired.

At five minutes past noon his faint breathing stopped altogether. Dr. Karen Schmidt happened to drop in a couple of minutes later and she confirmed that Ronald Ward Smith had died on Thursday, May 14th, 2015. It took another hour for the coroner to attend and sign a formal Death Certificate.

I followed the staff as they wheeled Old Ron downstairs where a vehicle from the cremation company was waiting to cart his corpse away. They advised that Ron would be processed immediately and that I could pick up his ashes later in the day at their office.

As callous as it may seem, I took out a final $2,000 from the bank machines before heading over to the crematorium.

Old Ron was dead but I was still alive and kicking.

Later in his apartment, I placed Old Ron's ashes on his beloved desk and then phoned Ben Van Huizen in Belleville as well as the beneficiaries to advise them all of Ron's peaceful death.

Finally I contacted Peter Long, the lawyer.

It was a very sad and tiring process delivering the news to everyone, and I felt depressed and completely alone after the final call had been made.

I had a pizza delivered for my supper and drank Old Ron's beer all evening.

I got on the internet and checked out a detailed map of Chicago as well as Google Earth. After a bit of fiddling around, I found the address where the Rushmore Arms had been in my world.

The same hotel did exist in this world but it was named the Hotel Maximus. I searched the hotel's website and found that the lovely hotel had been built in 2006 as the McMillan Ritz but the timing couldn't have been worse. Those original owners filed for bankruptcy in 2010 and the hotel continued to operate under the supervision of the trustee until the last day of December, 2014 when a sale to new owners finally closed. The following day it began operating as Hotel Maximus.

It was with a heavy heart and a stomach full of pizza and Old Ron's cheap beer when I stumbled into bed just before midnight.

Goodbye Old Ron. I wonder if you still exist in Sonia's world. Wouldn't that be a kick in my ass!

Perhaps you won Sonia after all while I'm stuck all alone in this alternate reality with very little money and a completely uncertain future.

CHAPTER 9 (Sonia's in Danger)

Precisely as had occurred during the previous two nights, Cecil appeared again on a cloud amidst a cacophony of static.

This time his face mirrored panic.

"They're going to murder Sonia in that other world," he blurted out, "and there's nothing I can do to stop them."

I felt an eerie combination of shock, terror and helplessness, stuck in the world where Sonia had already been eliminated.

"Are you certain?" was the only response I could muster.

"Yes, the evil creature is named Jarlon and his cohort is called Lorjan. They were arguing. From what I could gather, only Jarlon has the ability to spin itself into different shapes and enter his world, which they regard as their personal toys. Lorjan was strongly opposed to Jarlon's murder of Sonia in Jarlon's toy world and is now attempting to dissuade Jarlon from pursuing any further manipulation."

"Isn't the Sonia I knew protected while she's in her world?"

"That's what the two creatures are arguing about. Jarlon intends to rip a tiny temporary tear in the fabric separating the two spheres of reality. Jarlon will then enter his sphere, slip into Lorjan's sphere through the temporary portal, kill Sonia, return to his own sphere and finally come back to the creatures' shared home. I can tell from what I overheard that Jarlon is still trying to work out the details, so I have no idea when the murder will take place. Can you think of any way to stop it?"

"I doubt that it's possible to do anything at all. They have powers beyond anything you or I can even imagine. Do you think they're God?"

"That's preposterous! The God I worship encompasses pure love and compassion. He wouldn't callously murder an innocent woman to further some sick experiment. Besides, if these creatures were all-powerful, they'd be aware of my presence in their lair. They'd also know about these strange meetings you and I are having in some shared dream state."

"I wonder if there's some reason why I was transported from one world to the other. Cecil, do you have the ability to enter Sonia's dreams while she's in Lorjan's realm."

"I don't seem to have control over anything. I just appear in your presence and have no input into when, how or why."

"At the very least, the fact that we are meeting could indicate that some even higher power is now interfering with the creatures' plans. From my own bizarre experience I know that it is possible to slip from one world into the other because it happened to me. Some wave of energy knocked me out of my Sonia's world into the one you lived in. If God or something is attempting to help Sonia, then maybe your spirit will be allowed to slip into her world when the portal is open. If that happens, you might be able to warn Sonia in her dream."

"I'll try to find out more. The creatures are still frantically trying to pinpoint the source of the whole problem."

At that moment the crackling began and Cecil disappeared.

I woke up saddened, deflated and completely perplexed, wondering why I was even involved when everything was so utterly beyond my ability to intervene. Another mystery was why each of my shared dreams with Old Ron and now with Cecil all took place in Room 321 at the El Cortez in Las Vegas.

I toyed with the idea of returning to Las Vegas and staying again in the same room in the hope that I'd be transported back to Sonia's world so that I could somehow try to protect her.

With that thought in mind, I counted out all the money I'd been able to accumulate. In total I had $12,000 in Canadian funds and just under $23,000 in US cash. Sadly, with only the ID from a dead man, I was perplexed as to how I'd survive in this alternate world. I couldn't work here or do much of anything. The upscale life I'd loved so much was now out of my reach. I'd have to live frugally like Old Ron in order to make my funds last as long as possible.

That prospect felt incredibly unjust and unpalatable.

Since Old Ron was now deceased, I didn't have the nerve to try for one last bank machine withdrawal. As it was, the estate trustees and their lawyer would soon discover that I'd absconded with more than $30,000 of Old Ron's money in the few days I'd been in Laughlin.

There was a knock on my apartment door.

It was Liz Cotter again expressing her sincere condolences and making a request which alarmed me.

"Carl Kaufmann and I each got a phone call from Mr. Long earlier this morning, and he laid out for us what we need to do as Ron's estate trustees. Since Carl is so swamped at the hotel, he delegated me to obtain the information that the lawyer requires. I'm hoping that you can help me prepare a full inventory of Ron's assets."

Worried that I'd be branded a thief within hours and perhaps even arrested, I opted to delay the inevitable in order to allow myself time to come up with a plan to flee Laughlin forever.

"Of course I'll help you, Mrs. Cotter. I already provided Mr. Long with a preliminary list. I'll get right to work compiling an up-to-date complete inventory, and I'll print it off for you. That should get you started nicely with the legal work. Have you made an appointment yet to see Mr. Long?"

"Yes, we've agreed to see him at eleven o'clock on Tuesday morning."

"That's ideal. I'll make sure I have the information ready before then. Look, I'm going to have to return to South America shortly. You have another key for this apartment, don't you?"

"Yes."

"Feel free to enter the unit at any time whether I'm here or not. Ron's Will leaves all the contents to you personally. Since my brother's clothes fit me perfectly and I had to fly here on a moment's notice with only a sports bag, would you mind if I took whatever I need to get me back home?"

"Of course I don't mind, Don. Help yourself to anything you can use including any personal items you'd like for sentimental reasons."

I joked to myself that I'd already taken over $30,000 in cash for sentimental reasons, but I didn't disclose that morsel of information to Mrs. Cotter. I thanked her for being so gracious and she left.

In the afternoon I went around to every bank branch I could find and exchanged Canadian money for US cash. By the end of the afternoon I had successfully turned all but $850 into American funds. Since I only purchased $900 at a time, not a single teller asked me for identification or posed any prying questions. Only two of the tellers even asked me if I was a customer of that particular bank.

Small cash transactions are scandalously easy to make anonymously.

Most of the money was now in denominations of twenties or hundreds, but my cache was still somewhat bulky.

I had supper at a fast food outlet and then went shopping for a money belt. I found one at a specialty luggage shop. Next I went to a drug store and purchased a large roll of elastic medical bandage.

In the evening I completed a pretty complete inventory of Old Ron's estate and set out the approximate current balances of his various accounts that remained after my repeated raids on them.

In total the miser was worth about two and a half million, so all his beneficiaries would be paid their specific bequests while Mrs. Cotter and Carl Kaufmann would reap a sizeable haul from splitting the residue in the percentage shares I'd designated.

The Canadian and Ontario governments would also be happy with the income taxes and probate fees they'd confiscate.

It was a travesty that Old Ron had lived almost sixty-five years but had never managed to enjoy the lifestyle that such immense wealth could have afforded him.

Even more tragic was the poverty which had now befallen me and which would ensure that I'd be forced to lead a life of frugality. Old Ron loved living that way but I knew that I'd abhor it.

I printed off the detailed estate inventory and left it with a note to Mrs. Cotter in which I said that major problems had cropped up in South America, and that I had to leave in the middle of the night for Toronto in order to arrange a flight home.

I planned on leaving town either Sunday or Monday, wanting to be long gone by the time Liz and Carl met with the estate lawyer.

It was almost midnight by the time I hit the sack.

CHAPTER 10 (Mortal Danger)

No sooner had I drifted off to sleep when Cecil and I were immersed in another shared dream.

"Now you're in grave danger as well," he blurted out.

"How can that be?" I replied. "I've only been in this world for a week."

"The creatures have discovered that you just died in Jarlon's world but came out of your terminal coma in the other world and then met Sonia. Apparently that anomaly has caused the recent massive discrepancies between the two realms. Even more frightening, somehow they know that you've transported into Jarlon's world. They have no idea how that happened but I've learned from eavesdropping on the creatures that they can't track your movements now that you've transferred. Jarlon is coming to find and kill you tomorrow night. You've got to run for your life."

"What possible chance do I have running from it? I'd rather stand my ground and fight. If I'm able to kill this Jarlon when it comes for me, then Sonia might be safe back in the other world."

"Don't ask me how, but an escape plan has been conveyed to me. Apparently I'm the medium being used by some third party, perhaps even God himself, to thwart the creatures' intentions. The creatures can track Sonia in her world and Jarlon intends to insert itself into Old Ron's apartment tomorrow night in order to kill you because that's where Jarlon expects that you'll be. That's why you've got to run and hide. Since Jarlon can't track you, then the only way he can find you is the old-fashioned way, like a bounty hunter searching for a convict."

"How does that help Sonia survive?"

"My beautiful daughter is doomed if she remains in Lorjan's world because her movements can be monitored there. Jarlon intends to murder her as soon as he kills you. Apparently if you flee and elude Jarlon, then doing so will buy Sonia some valuable time. By the time Jarlon gives up searching for you on Saturday night, Sonia will already have had sufficient time to escape."

"Where can she possibly go if the creatures can track her?"

"As soon as I leave this dream with you, apparently I'll be taken into a dream in the other world with Sonia where I can warn her to go immediately to a specific location where she can be transported into Jarlon's world during the moment when Jarlon opens the portal between the two worlds. Like you, Sonia will need all her wits to escape from Jarlon, but the creatures won't be able to trace her in Jarlon's world."

My heart began racing inside the dream. There was a slim chance that Sonia and I could reunite.

"Where will I be able to find Sonia?"

"I simply don't know. At this moment I'm not privy to where she'll land in Jarlon's world."

"How can Sonia and I possibly find each other?"

"I can't answer that except to emphasize that both of you will have to steer clear of Laughlin, Las Vegas and Chicago because those are the locations that Jarlon will be watching for you if you and Sonia do manage to hide."

"Can I give you a rendezvous location so that you can tell Sonia?"

"No, my instincts are warning me to avoid any specific knowledge about that. I feel that it's possible that Jarlon will find me and torture any information out of me."

"Sonia and I will never find each other without some clue."

Cecil went completely mute and motionless on his dream cloud. I had no idea what was happening to him.

After a moment, he revived.

"I've been instructed that you must give me a cryptic message to convey to Sonia, something that only she and you could decipher."

I wracked my brain for some clue that Sonia would understand but that would be meaningless to our pursuer. My recent dream provided me with the answer, and I blurted out, "A flower for my beautiful shipmate."

The static began and Cecil began to vaporize but he managed to say, "Good luck, Ron. Please keep my Sonia safe and happy. This is the last time you and I will communicate. Somehow I know that the more changes you cause, the more difficult it will be for the creatures to manipulate either world, and at some point they will completely lose their limited ability to influence either realm."

Cecil was gone and I immediately woke up. It was one o'clock in the morning. I quickly showered and shaved.

I put on the money belt, which was also elasticized and designed to be worn around the lower chest area. I hid the belt by wrapping it with medical tape as if I'd sustained a rib injury.

Then I got dressed and packed my sports bag with clothing and other small items which I guessed would be useful for my escape. I found a baseball cap with a small Las Vegas casino logo and put it on as a flimsy attempt at disguise.

I quietly locked the apartment door and then slid the key back under the door. Having already written the note to Mrs. Cotter saved me valuable time.

Once I was outside in the dark, I found myself unsure as to what my next move should be. I'd already rejected the notion of stealing Old Ron's car and driving it to Windsor, realizing that doing so would disclose to both Jarlon and the police which direction I was headed. My note to Mrs. Cotter said that I was going to Toronto and I didn't want to leave any contrary evidence.

Having no experience with being on the run, I walked surreptitiously toward a truck stop I knew was on the southwest end of town. There was virtually no traffic on the way, but to be safe I ducked behind bushes or trees whenever I spotted a vehicle in the distance.

Once I arrived at the large truck stop, I pondered how I could bum a ride to Windsor or Sarnia, the two nearest border crossings into America.

I sauntered inside, sat on a bench near the men's washroom for a while, and then stood up and perused a large wall map of Ontario.

Luck was with me because a fellow in his forties came out of the washroom and stopped to ask me what I was looking for.

"I was supposed to meet a buddy at this truck stop to catch a ride to Windsor," I lied, "but he didn't show up. I'm just looking at the map trying to decide whether it's too far to walk."

"Oh, it's way too far to hoof it, but tell you what, I'm going through Windsor. You can ride with me if you want."

"That would be fantastic. I didn't know what I was going to do. Thank you so much."

As we walked to his vehicle, my savior introduced himself as Russell. I shook his hand and said that my name was Hal. The ride turned out to be a big rig.

As Russell maneuvered it out of the service center and on to the highway, he used my presence as his grievance board.

"It's been one brute of a day, Hal. I left Montreal early this morning and made stops in Toronto, Kitchener, London and Laughlin. I'm beat and thankful to have your company for this last short haul because even the coffee I just had might not have kept me awake. After I drop off the last of my load at the depot, I'll grab three or four hours sleep in the cab while they load me back up for my next run. I've been trucking for seventeen years and it's a bitch of a life. After two divorces, I'm back on my own and practically starting over."

Knowing next to nothing about transportation, I wanted to keep Russell talking. The less information I divulged to anyone, the better my chances would be to keep my escape route secret. I asked Russell to tell me about the places he'd been and some of the troubles he'd encountered along the way.

That little ploy worked like a charm and Russell didn't even stop to take a breath in between stories. When we hit the outskirts of the city of Windsor an hour later, Russell asked where I'd like to be dropped off.

"I don't want to barge in on my friends in the middle of the night. Do you know any place on your way that's open all night and has internet access?"

"I know just the spot. There's a small truck stop up ahead that's got exactly what you're looking for. It's right on this road."

Sure enough, a few minutes later Russell stopped to let me out. I thanked him for the ride and told him to get a good sleep.

At the restaurant I ate a full early breakfast and then purchased a few hours of internet time on one of the desktop computers.

I was concerned about how I could cross the border into Detroit with the least chance of detection. As a last resort I could purchase a bus ticket but assumed that doing so might make it too easy for Jarlon to track me.

An interesting idea struck me and I began surfing for tourist day trips from Windsor to Detroit. Several places offered same-day casino trips across the border to the big casinos in Detroit. I almost selected one of them until I read the terms and conditions. Carry-on bags were strictly prohibited as a deterrent to prevent travelers from using the cheap or sometimes free casino junkets as inexpensive transportation from one city to the other.

Overnight trips were also offered. I spent considerable time examining those and chose three that seemed most promising.

I looked at the Windsor city map on-line and noted where each bus line or travel office was located.

For purposes of anonymity I selected a tour leaving at ten this morning with accommodation at a small private motel in Detroit. Although this was the cheapest tour, what really attracted me to it was the tiny size of both the bus line, which operated only three coaches, and the motel which was an older, single-storey privately-owned business.

The bus office opened at nine o'clock and the bus for the overnight tour departed right from that office which was within easy walking distance from this truck stop.

Just in case that bus tour was cancelled or already full, I jotted down the details for two other possibilities.

I killed time on the computer until quarter to eight when I walked to the bus line office which turned out to be a single desk in a travel agency located in a small strip plaza.

When they opened their doors just before nine o'clock, I walked in to inquire if there were any openings left on the overnight tour to the Detroit casino.

I was in luck. I paid cash and confirmed to the woman that I had a valid Canadian passport. She didn't even ask for my name, which pleased me. Even though I was a novice at being on the run, common sense indicated that the fewer people to whom I had to disclose my name, the more difficult it would be for some alien assassin to catch me.

Half an hour later the small shuttle bus pulled into the plaza and I hopped on board. There were only twenty-three seats on the bus and by the time we departed at ten o'clock, seven seats remained empty.

I was very nervous when we approached US customs, worried sick that my passport from the other world would be rejected. My fear was that getting into the USA would entail a much more stringent examination of my documentation than had occurred when I'd entered Canada a week ago. I'd almost switched that passport

73

with the valid one I found in Old Ron's apartment in this world, but had decided that it would be safer to leave the right one in Laughlin.

I needn't have been concerned. Just like coming in by bus from Canada, a customs agent came on this casino bus and visually examined everyone's identification.

When he got to me and asked if I was carrying more than $10,000, I smiled and smoothly lied. "Not today, but hopefully I'll have a different answer for you tomorrow when we come back from the casino."

"You're living in fantasyland," the agent replied with a huge grin on his face.

All of the passengers passed inspection and at precisely quarter past ten we crossed the bridge into Detroit.

Checking into the small motel was also extremely informal. I used the name Arnie Ward.

The bus driver instructed us to put our things in our rooms and get back on the bus at eleven o'clock to be taken to the casino. He suggested that for those passengers who didn't yet possess a casino player's card, it was wise to obtain one in order to receive a coupon book for discount meals and other specials.

As we later disembarked at the casino entrance, the driver announced, "Remember people, I'll be back here at four o'clock, seven, ten and finally one in the morning in case anyone wants to go back to the motel. I'll also leave the motel to return to this casino at fifteen minutes before each of those hours. Feel free to hop on and off at any time."

The room had been clean but very basic. I had put my sports bag on the bed, showered quickly and then jumped back on the bus.

Not entirely certain as to the next phase of my grand escape plan, I decided to stay the night in the motel and try to formulate a strategy to continue my journey with the least chance of being detected.

My ultimate destination was San Antonio, Texas. That was the location I hoped Sonia would decipher from my cryptic message. We had spent several nights in that lovely city and had cruised along the Riverwalk canals each day in little tour boats.

On one of those days I had given Sonia a long-stemmed red rose and lovingly gushed, "A flower for my beautiful shipmate." Since that precise moment had been a part of my recent dream, I surmised that perhaps the recollection had been a bit of divine intervention rather than just a handy coincidence.

I wore my cap well down over my face in the casino and found a bank of slot machines in a somewhat secluded corner at the rear of the casino. Sonia and I had both detested gambling when we were in Las Vegas but she mentioned that Old Ron actually loved the slots, especially a game called Caveman Keno in which he bet just one quarter at a time. She added that the free drinks he got as a slot player more than compensated for the bit of money he lost to the one-armed bandits.

The machine I sat at didn't have that particular game but it did have other keno games, so I inserted a five dollar bill and began playing.

It was about as exciting as watching paint dry so I played very slowly while I wracked my brain for some inspiration as to how to get to San Antonio in secret.

From time to time other players would sit down at the machines beside me. Some of them were quite chatty. I began asking each player where they were from, hoping to discover someone who was heading either west or south.

Sick of the slots, I caught the bus back to the motel at four o'clock and ate supper at a restaurant across the road.

Back in the room, I studied a map of America which I'd found in Old Ron's apartment. At quarter to seven I caught the shuttle bus back to the casino.

This time I began chatting up a hot prospect.

Moe Enright, a chap about my age who had driven to Detroit from northern Michigan, was staying tonight at the hotel attached to this casino. Tomorrow morning he was continuing on to Indianapolis. I didn't mention that I was Canadian.

We had a long friendly chat about assorted topics. When Moe eventually asked me where I was headed, I answered, "I'm staying overnight at a motel near here and tomorrow I'll check out the bus schedules to St. Louis."

I was hoping for an offer of a ride as far as Indianapolis but nothing was forthcoming.

When Moe came back from a washroom break, I was contemplating coming right out and asking if I could bum a ride, but fortunately he beat me to the punch and offered to get me as far as Indianapolis tomorrow if I was interested.

"That would be great, Moe. It'll make my journey simpler and much faster. I'd like to pay for the gas and meals if you'll permit me."

That appeared to please Moe and we arranged to meet at the casino front entrance tomorrow morning at eight o'clock when my motel shuttle made its first drop-off.

I returned to the motel on the ten o'clock run and set the rocm alarm for seven on Sunday morning, pleased that my escape plan was progressing nicely.

CHAPTER 11 (Sonia's Surprise)

Sonia Poniecki unlocked her high-rise condominium apartment door and immediately slumped on the sofa, almost consumed by grief and worry.

Her father had just died this afternoon after a difficult ten days following his massive stroke.

For the past several hours, Sonia and her two daughters had consoled Bernice and had assisted her in sorting out things at both the hospital and the funeral home.

Sonia had wanted to stay overnight at her mother's apartment, but Bernice insisted that Sonia go back to her own condo in case Ron called.

The grief over Cecil's death was bad enough, but added to that was the intense worry Sonia felt over her beloved Ron. He had promised to email and phone her regularly in order to keep her abreast of his long drive to Chicago.

Ron was already several days overdue and Sonia hadn't heard a word from him. That was so out of character.

She berated herself for flying back to Chicago alone, but Ron had calmly assured her that he and Old Ron would have no difficulty driving to Chicago. It was clear that something dreadful had happened.

Sonia had phoned the El Cortez in Las Vegas a few days earlier and confirmed that Ron had checked out on the 7th. Even that tidbit of information was disturbing because Ron had promised to leave Las Vegas three days before that.

Somehow the two Rons must have encountered some communication glitch which delayed their departure by three days.

Sonia berated herself for not analyzing the situation more carefully when Karen had called about Cecil's stroke. It would have been so much simpler for both she and Ron to have flown to Chicago together. They could have paid for the El Cortez room for an additional week and none of this would now be happening.

It was too late for recriminations and second guessing.

Sonia poured herself a glass of wine and sat on the sofa, crying softly. Her world was being turned upside down by these recent events.

So many things had gone wrong. Sonia's answering machine had broken when she tried to reconnect it to her phone when she first arrived in Chicago, and she hadn't had a chance to purchase a new one. Sonia had been too busy ferrying her mother to and from the hospital. There'd been no time for shopping.

At half past ten she went to bed, still sobbing and overwhelmed. Within a few minutes, exhaustion overtook her and Sonia drifted off to sleep.

The next thing Sonia knew, she was sitting on a small cloud. She looked around in confusion and discovered that she was back in Room 321 at the El Cortez. This was so strange! The two versions of Ron had met in shared dreams in this very setting. Now it appeared that Ron was about to communicate with Sonia in the same way.

Sonia was aware of a crackling sound as another cloud began forming across the hotel room.

Instead of Ron appearing, it was Sonia's father.

"Dad, what's happening?"

"I don't have time to explain much, darling. Please just listen and trust me. There are two parallel worlds observed by two alien creatures. In an attempt to increase their entertainment quotient, one of them murdered you last December in the world where I lived. I died from a stroke induced by intense grief on March 30th. Am I still alive in your world?"

"No, Dad; you just died this afternoon. I can't make sense of anything you're telling me."

"You've just got to trust me, sweetie. Your boyfriend Ron inexplicably got transported from your world into mine, and to his great dismay discovered that in my world you were dead. I've been sharing dreams with him for the past few nights. The creatures have just discovered that in my world Ron never came out of his coma in Canada. In fact, that version of Ron just died a couple of days ago and your boyfriend was at his bedside. The creatures also know that the Ron you know is now permanently stuck in my world. One of the creatures, named Jarlon is going tomorrow night to kill Ron in Laughlin, but in a dream earlier tonight I was able to warn Ron to flee. Jarlon is also coming to murder you. You've got to leave Chicago as soon as you wake up. Don't use any credit cards and don't leave any trace of where you go. Try to disguise yourself."

"But where can I go, Dad?"

"Get yourself to the southwest service entrance of the Rushmore Arms Hotel. You'll be transported to the other world but I don't know where it is that you'll arrive. It could be anywhere. Ron has given me a secret message that only you should understand. He said, 'A flower for my beautiful shipmate,' and I pray to God that you know from that where he wants to meet up with you. Don't tell me where that is, but can you figure out from that message where he wants you to go?"

"Yes Dad, I understand Ron's message. Can I leave some sort of note for Mom and the girls?"

"I guess so but Jarlon might intercept it if you leave it lying around your apartment."

"Where exactly are you, Dad?"

"I really don't know. Some higher power seems to be assisting me in communicating first with Ron and now with you, and I've been given the ability to eavesdrop on the alien creatures without their knowledge. I'm certain that whatever entity is helping me is doing so to protect you and Ron and perhaps to put a stop to the creatures' ability to interfere with the two worlds."

"I still can't make any sense out of what you're telling me, Dad."

"Apparently Ron wasn't supposed to emerge from the coma in either world. His unplanned existence coupled with his meeting up with you has somehow completely upended the experiment."

"What experiment are you talking about?"

"Jarlon decided to kill one random person, who turned out to be you, in his world for the sole purpose of observing whatever changes your murder would have. The combination of Ron waking up from the coma and then meeting you has completely upended that experiment and has caused rapidly escalating differences between the two realms. Jarlon believes that killing you and Ron is the only way to salvage the situation and retain his limited control over the parallel worlds."

"How can I recognize Jarlon?"

"I don't know, sweetie. Please disguise yourself well. I'm so pleased that you still exist. I've missed you terribly. Remember, the key to breaking the creatures' power to affect the two worlds is to cause as many changes as you can whether you find Ron or not."

"What will happen to you, Dad?"

"I don't know, but I sense that some higher power is on my side and has kept me in a state of limbo solely to help you and Ron evade Jarlon's vile intentions. I'm hoping that my job will be done as soon as you've slipped into the other world, and that I'll be taken to my Maker. Good luck, my darling Sonia. I love you."

The static returned and Cecil disappeared.

Sonia woke up immediately.

She was absolutely convinced that what she had just experienced was no mere dream, but how could she abandon her mother and her daughters in this realm?"

Unsure as to what to do, Sonia showered and dressed in casual clothes and running shoes. Then she rummaged around her closets and found an oversized purse almost the size of a department store shopping bag. She quickly packed it with extra clothing and other items as if she were going off on a weekend jaunt.

Removing all her credit cards from her wallet, Sonia counted out her cash, which totaled less than $200. She found another few dollars of change in a drawer.

Sonia really had no idea how to disguise herself, but tried wrapping a scarf tightly around her hair. That helped along with applying no makeup or lipstick.

Not requiring prescription eyeglasses, Sonia found a pair of dark-rimmed glasses with clear lenses in a drawer, and that definitely changed her appearance.

Her next task was composing a letter to her family, and that proved difficult indeed. The whole scenario described by her father was preposterous.

In the end she wrote a note in her own handwriting concocting a story that Ron had been waiting for her when she got home last evening. Dangerous men were trying to kill him and he was frantic that they would try to kidnap Sonia in order to force Ron to give himself up. She implored her family not to contact the police and to tell anyone who asked that Sonia had continued on an extensive driving trip. Sonia added that she and Ron might have to live underground for several years, perhaps even permanently. She wrote how much she loved her family but that Sonia wanted to be with Ron. She added that Karen and Nancy had her signed power of attorney and that they had Sonia's permission to sell all her assets and transfer the proceeds to themselves.

Sonia put the note in an envelope, addressed it to her mother and found a postage stamp. She would post the letter in a mail box on her way to the Rushmore Arms.

Her watch showed that it was just half past midnight. Sonia left most of her keys in the apartment but kept one spare key. Deeming it expedient to avoid the elevators, she quietly made her way to the stairwell, walked down to the parking garage, waited in hiding for a few minutes and then snuck outside after a car entered.

Briskly she strode out to the road and crossed to the other side. Then she walked about ten minutes until she came to a major road where she posted her letter and waited at a bus stop.

After twenty minutes a bus finally pulled up and the driver told Sonia where to transfer to get downtown.

Time was elapsing and it was more than an hour before she finally stepped off another bus in front of the Rushmore Arms. Sonia walked around to the southwest service entrance and waited.

If I get swooped off to the other world, Sonia thought, then so be it. If nothing happens than I'll grab a taxi back to my apartment and get back in with my spare key. If that latter scenario occurs, then Mom and the girls will get a big chuckle out of my bizarre dream when I tell them what I was doing in the middle of the night. I've always been such a sensible girl but tonight I'm acting like a lunatic.

Sonia sat waiting near the service entrance clutching her bag and wondering how long she should wait before determining that she'd experienced nothing but a strange dream and head back home. She decided to wait until five o'clock assuming that no one showed up before then to shoo away this crazy bag lady.

About an hour after she arrived, something unseen flowed over her and pushed her onto her side.

When a dizzy Sonia righted herself a moment later, something was amiss. The configuration of her surroundings was similar but something seemed vaguely different.

84

Gingerly, Sonia stood up and made her way to the front of the hotel.

To her profound amazement, the large neon sign advertising the Rushmore Arms now proclaimed "Hotel Maximus."

Her father had been telling the truth. Sonia was now in a different world but still on the run from scary creatures.

She walked back to the bus stop and within ten minutes a bus arrived. This time Sonia opted to go as far south on Lakeshore Drive as the bus system would take her.

It took three transfers and the payment of one additional fare, but at five o'clock she was finally dropped off in Joliet. It was still pitch black outside and the last bus driver had indicated that there was an all-night restaurant about a ten minute walk to the west.

When Sonia found the spot, the diner turned out to be a popular place for truckers and there were three different rigs parked there.

She sat at the counter and ordered breakfast and a coffee while trying to work up a strategy to put more distance between her and the danger in Chicago.

When Sonia was about half-way through demolishing the big plate of sausage, eggs, hash browns and toast, a loud boisterous woman entered the restaurant and plunked herself down at the adjoining stool.

"Nothing wrong with your appetite, honey," the woman quipped.

Sonia smiled and replied, "I had no idea the portions were so huge. It's very tasty though."

"I'm just teasing, honey. I'll be ordering the same thing. I've got a whole day of trucking ahead of me and I need some fuel. Where are you headed?"

Sonia quickly concocted a cover story.

"I've just escaped an abusive situation, so I'm trying to get as far away from here as I can before the bastard wakes up and comes looking for me."

"Are you driving?"

"No, I haven't yet figured out how I'm traveling. I caught a city bus this far but I'm afraid to buy a ticket anywhere at a proper bus or train station. That's the first place he'll look."

The woman didn't respond right away and Sonia realized that she was being sized up.

Finally the woman, sufficiently reassured, said, "You're welcome to ride with me. I'm going as far as Tulsa but you can get off any place between here and there. By the way, my name's Barb Allan."

"You're a lifesaver, Barb. I'm Justine and I'd be thrilled to hitch a ride with you."

CHAPTER 12 (San Antonio)

I checked out of the motel and caught the first shuttle of the morning back to the casino. I told the bus driver that a friend was taking me back to Canada so I wouldn't be on his return bus later in the day.

He thanked me for the information, adding that often people didn't forewarn him and that caused delays returning to Windsor as the whole bus waited around for at least ten minutes after the scheduled departure time, which made everyone angry.

Moe was already waiting nearby as I stepped off the bus, and he had just finished breakfast in the casino restaurant.

I lied that I'd eaten a free breakfast in my motel, and Moe seemed pleased that we could set out right away.

As with Russell the trucker, I let Moe do most of the talking. He was a retired teacher and football coach, but had been working the past week in Sault Ste. Marie as a consultant for a college football team conducting early tryouts for their next season.

Moe proudly mentioned that he had played part of one season for San Diego in the old American Football League and three full seasons for the Hamilton Tiger Cats in the Canadian Football League before suffering a career-ending knee injury. Moe then attended teachers' college in his home state of Indiana as a mature student.

We stopped for gas once and I insisted on paying for the fill-up.

I was careful not to disclose my last name or my eventual destination. I said that I was originally from upper New York State but now lived near St. Louis, and that I had worked in an insurance agency until retiring last year.

The entire trip to Indianapolis took only four hours, and Moe dropped me off right at the main bus terminal.

Looking over my map of the USA and the bus schedules, there were many choices to get to San Antonio.

Not wanting to make my itinerary too easy to recreate, I decided to let timing dictate my next travel route.

There was a bus going west to St. Louis in forty minutes and another departing for Louisville, Nashville and finally New Orleans at two o'clock.

I opted to head south, figuring that in the highly unlikely event that Jarlon ever found Moe Enright, the creature would be given a bum steer that I was going to St. Louis.

I purchased my ticket and grabbed a late lunch at a restaurant near the terminal.

It was an incredibly long and tiring day and night, and I had to change buses at Nashville and again at Birmingham.

I sat alone near the back of the buses most of the way and only had a seatmate once, the whole of which time I either pretended to be asleep or actually did nod off.

Finally at three o'clock in the morning, the bus pulled into the New Orleans depot. The first bus west wasn't leaving until five o'clock so I purchased a ticket to Houston and waited.

That trip took another five hours since the coach made stops at all the moderately sized cities along the way.

There was only an additional hour's wait in Houston until a bus left for San Antonio, and it made no stops at all. A few minutes past two o'clock in the afternoon, I stepped off the bus at my final destination.

I was as certain as I could be that no one, not even Jarlon, could trace my trail here. The only nagging misgiving I had was whether Jarlon with his superhuman intelligence could decipher my cryptic message to Sonia.

My thoughts had been with Sonia during my arduous time on the buses, and I wondered whether Cecil had been successful in warning her to flee and if by some miracle Sonia had by now been transported into this world.

My plan was to find a hotel room on the Riverwalk and wait in that area until I spotted Sonia. I had no idea how long it would take her to make it to San Antonio and I suspected that she wouldn't have the ability to be as furtive in slinking out of Chicago as I'd been in leaving Laughlin.

Then again, Cecil didn't know where Sonia would land once she was transported into this world. She might find herself in Las Vegas or even somewhere on the other side of the planet.

I suspected that, since I had landed in exactly the same location, Sonia also would most likely find herself in the alternate Chicago.

Hoping to disguise myself more completely, and not really knowing how much deception was required, I decided to find a motel room well away from the Riverwalk for tonight and use that opportunity to concoct a more permanent disguise.

I purchased a street map of San Antonio at the bus station and studied it while I ate a late lunch.

I asked the waitress where I might find an inexpensive motel, and she mentioned that there were several older motels on Commerce Street. On the way there I passed a costume and novelty store so I ducked inside and looked around.

They carried a decent selection of wigs, beards and mustaches.

After trying on a few in front of a mirror, I made my selection and paid the bored clerk for my purchases. I put on my new disguise in the privacy of an alley just up the street from the store.

Suddenly I was transformed into a long-haired hippie with matching beard and mustache. The disguise was so effective that I was sure that even Sonia couldn't recognize me.

About ten minutes later I came across some motels and rented a room in one of them that advertised a single rate of only $30.

It was so dumpy and depressing that I was convinced that even Old Ron would approve of my choice.

I showered, cleaned myself up and walked the mile or so over to the Riverwalk area.

Strolling around, I located the main commencement point for the canal tours and decided to find a hotel room near there.

After at least an hour of evaluating the possible options, I selected a small three-storey inn somewhat in need of refurbishment. I waltzed up to the young female desk clerk who informed me that the hotel was offering a special rate for stays of at least three nights. I was able to book a room commencing tomorrow night on the second floor overlooking the Riverwalk. I paid the rate in cash and got a receipt. The clerk advised that I could pick up the key tomorrow after eleven o'clock.

I sat on a bench near the boat tour ticket kiosk and looked for Sonia, but was unsuccessful. I realized that it was highly unlikely that she could have made it to San Antonio as quickly as I had.

On the way back to my seedy little motel, I purchased a six-pack of beer and a submarine sandwich, opting to stay in my room for the evening.

CHAPTER 13 (Sonia's Adventure)

   After breakfast Sonia followed Barb out to
the big semi, her heart soaring with relief
knowing that a great distance was soon to
separate her from the alien assassin.
   Barb was extremely chatty and spent the
first hour talking about life on the road.
Eventually Barb brought the conversation
around to Sonia's predicament.
   "How do you think you're going to survive
now that you've left Chicago?" Barb asked
tactfully.
   "At this precise moment I'm so thrilled to
have escaped that I don't even care. Please
forgive me if I don't provide any specific
details, but my husband is quite wealthy and
totally ruthless. I know he'll send private
detectives on my trail, and it's possible that
they'll discover that I was talking to you in
that diner and track me through you. Do you
have any maps I can study?"
   "Of course honey; there's a whole bunch of
older maps in the glove box in front of you. I
tend to use the GPS now instead of the maps."
   Sonia pulled out some of the maps and found
one showing the entire USA. After a few
minutes of silence, she made her decision how
to further hide her route.
   "Barb, I assure you that I'm not in any
trouble with the police or anything like that,
but my husband is truly insane. Hopefully
you'll never be questioned about whether
you've ever met me, but if they do discover
that I hitched a ride with you, it would be
much safer for me if you lied and told them

that you dropped me off in St. Louis because I said I had to head west to the Denver area."

"No problem, Justine. Are you just going to drop off the face of the earth?"

"I truly hope so. My life literally depends on it now that I've left him."

"Were you able to grab enough money to get by with?"

"No, he never let me near money. He had absolute control over everything, but I don't care now. My freedom is worth more than a truckload of gold. I know I'll get by just fine. I was able to squirrel away almost $200 which actually makes me feel rich. I'm smart and innovative despite the countless putdowns I've endured over the years. Look, that's enough about me. I want to hear all about your life."

Sonia listened in fascination as Barb related her life story about years of minimum wage jobs, mostly part time, until she finally found a small trucking company which was so desperate for drivers that it paid for her training two years ago. Now Barb was making a decent wage and loved the adventure that a truck driver's life offered.

Well past St. Louis, Barb announced that she'd be stopping soon to use the washroom.

"I don't want to appear too paranoid, Barb, but I probably shouldn't be seen with you. Is there anywhere we can stop that's somewhat private?"

"Sure; are you hungry?"

"No, but I would like to find a washroom soon."

"There's a rest area about fifty miles from here, so we can stop there. We'll be totally discreet, go in separately and time it so that it's empty and no one sees us."

That ploy worked like a charm and Sonia was certain that her brief visit to those facilities was carried out in absolute secrecy.

Two hours later, Barb announced that she needed to grab something to eat at a truck stop just past Springfield.

"Would you prefer to stay in the truck?"

"Yes, I think that would be safer."

"I'll park in a spot where no one will even know you're in the cab."

"Thank you so much, Barb. If I give you some money, will you bring me back a sandwich?"

"I won't accept your money, honey. The food will be my treat. I usually eat at this place on my Tulsa runs because it gives me a chance to eat and then walk around a bit to relax my ass. I hope you don't mind if I take my time."

"Of course not, Barb. Take all the time you need."

An hour later Barb returned with a sandwich, doughnut and juice for Sonia who ate while they were back on Interstate 44. After another ninety minutes they were entering Oklahoma which was a toll road. Barb suggested that Sonia duck down while they passed the ticket booth to ensure that no one could see her.

By four o'clock they hit the eastern outskirts of Tulsa.

"My depot is on the west end of Tulsa, and that's where I dump this trailer and get hooked up with another one which I then take east to Detroit. Where would you like me to let you off, Justine?"

"Anywhere that's safe for you to stop," Sonia answered. "I'm so eternally grateful to you for offering me this ride, not to mention

94

buying my lunch. I'm sure that I'll be fine now."

Barb pulled in to a truck stop in order to let her rider off in an isolated section of the property, and handed her two maps, one of the city of Tulsa and the other of Oklahoma.

"Take these maps, Justine. You need to know exactly where you are. Good luck in your new life. I'll be thinking of you and wishing that you've found happiness."

Sonia hugged the kindly woman and furtively walked back to the busy portion of the service center. Then she turned around and watched Barb's rig pull away back onto the highway.

Sonia studied the map of Tulsa and concluded that she should try to leave such a large city before it got dark. She entered the restaurant building and phoned the bus station. The fares to San Antonio were more than her meager stash of cash would allow.

Hitchhiking was a possibility but Sonia was concerned that hundreds of drivers would see her as they passed by. That was exactly the opposite of the low visibility that Sonia needed.

Expecting that it was highly unlikely that another opportunity like Barb would fall into her lap, Sonia decided to be more proactive.

She sized up potential targets and approached her first choice, a very poorly-dressed young woman who was looking at a map.

"Excuse me, miss. I just got dropped off here and I'm heading for Dallas. I'd be pleased to pay for your gas if you're heading south. I'm also a good navigator if you need assistance interpreting the map."

The girl looked suspiciously at Sonia but didn't reply immediately. Finally she said, "I'm only going as far as Durant which is about 150 miles south of here. If you give me twenty bucks and spring for some doughnuts and coffee, you can ride with me."

"It's a deal," Sonia smiled. "What kind of doughnuts do you like?"

"Let's go see what they've got," the girl replied.

Sonia purchased half a dozen assorted and two large coffees and then handed the girl a twenty dollar bill.

"If it's okay with you, let's eat them in the car once I put a bit of gas in the tank," the girl suggested. "It'll take us about three hours to get to Durant and I don't want to drive in the dark. My name's Leslie Lewis."

"I'm Gloria," Sonia answered. "I'm ready to hit the road and I really appreciate the lift. I called the bus station from here but the fare was too expensive."

She walked with Leslie to a beat-up old rust bucket and off they drove.

Leslie was very talkative and self-centered, not asking Sonia a single question. The young girl was twenty-two and trying to juggle two minimum-wage jobs as a maid in two separate hotels near the highway a couple of miles west of Durant. Leslie shared the rent of a dilapidated old farmhouse next door to one of the motels with two other hotel maids. Money was perpetually scarce and she was living hand to mouth.

"The only reason I've even got a car today is because my older brother loaned it to me for the day. He bought it for fifty bucks last month and managed to get it running without spending another cent on it, so Harley kept it as a spare. He's a mechanic and a pretty good one. Anyways, I had to go up to Tulsa this morning for a medical test so he let me borrow it. I know what you mean by the cost of a bus ticket. The twenty bucks you gave me really helps me out. I wasn't sure I had enough dough in my purse to get me back home."

When Leslie tired of complaining about her crappy jobs, Sonia asked if she had a boyfriend.

That topic led to Leslie bad-mouthing men in general and Durant guys in particular as she described the miserable luck she'd encountered in trying to find and hold on to a boyfriend.

The funniest thing Leslie blurted out during the entire ride was when she proclaimed in all seriousness, "Right at this moment I'm in between losers."

Sonia laughed out loud and commiserated that hopefully the next guy who came along would be a keeper.

The three hours passed very quickly and it was almost eight o'clock when Leslie dropped Sonia off in downtown Durant before returning the car to her brother and having him drive her back to the farmhouse.

It was still light outside but Sonia was getting quite apprehensive about where she might sleep. At least the weather was cooperating just in case Sonia had to rough it outdoors tonight.

She asked directions to the bus station but discovered that it was closed until Monday morning.

Sonia walked past a small restaurant that was not only open but quite busy. There was a "HELP WANTED" sign in the window. Sonia decided to treat herself to a coffee and see if another opportunity presented itself. She was quite exhausted, having slept for only an hour last night before waking up after Cecil had appeared in her dream.

The waitress, a woman somewhat older than Sonia, was run right off her feet as Sonia sat at an empty stool up at the counter. It appeared that the woman was running the whole show by herself and was becoming a bit testy, as she barked at one of the customers, "Hold your damn horses, Hank. I've got to cook the bloody food before I can bring it to you."

When the woman on one of her mad dashes spotted Sonia at the counter, she composed herself and politely asked, "What can I get you, dear?"

"You can hire me for a couple of days. I need a place to stay for a night or two and you seem to be in dire need of a waitress this evening."

"Have you worked as a waitress before?"

"Not since I was in school, but I'm smart, clean, trustworthy and, more importantly, I'm right here, right now. You'd be doing me a great favor. I'm Kate."

"It's a deal. My name's Flo. Come with me. You can wash up in the kitchen and grab an apron. I'd better cook and handle the cash register. You can take the orders and deliver the food and beer."

Sonia washed her hands thoroughly and quickly made herself useful to Flo. The food orders soon dried up as the mostly male crowd quaffed their Saturday night beer.

Several of the older men flirted with Sonia and tried to get her phone number. The fatigue never returned until after one o'clock when Flo shooed out the customers and closed up the restaurant. There had been no time during the entire evening to chat with Flo.

"I own this portion of the building and have my apartment in the back. You've been a great help tonight, Kate and you're welcome to crash on my couch. I'm sorry we haven't had a chance to get acquainted, but Saturday night is my busiest time. I open the place at six in the morning for the breakfast crowd. Can you work tomorrow?"

"Certainly, and I'll be forever grateful for the roof over my head tonight. Maybe tomorrow I'll get a chance to tell you why I was homeless and desperate tonight. I'm so beat right now. I've been up for the past twenty-four hours."

"I'm beat myself. My regular waitress quit on Thursday morning and ran off with her new boyfriend, so I've been a one-woman band since then. Follow me."

Sonia walked behind Flo through a door into a small apartment behind the restaurant.

"Here's a spare sheet, pillow and blanket, Kate. In the morning I'll get showered and dressed first and then I'll wake you up. Sleep well and thanks for the help tonight."

Sonia couldn't even begin to assess her current situation or think about whether Ron had also been able to flee the creatures. She was dead to the world within twenty seconds of lying down on the sofa.

CHAPTER 14 (Full Disclosure)

Sonia woke in a groggy fog when she heard a woman's voice calling, "Time to get up, Kate."

Sonia groaned and sat up, at first confused but quickly she came to terms with reality.

"The bathroom's all yours, Kate. I'm going to get the restaurant up and running. Just come in when you're dressed and ready to work. The customers won't start flowing in until about six-thirty but the Sunday morning crowd is generally large. Did you sleep well?"

"Yes, but not nearly long enough. I should be ready to help you in about thirty minutes."

Over the course of the day, Sonia really got to know Flo and what a difficult life she'd had, working such long days. She was a widow with no pension and had been operating the restaurant on her own for the past eight years, ever since the day her husband slumped over and died on the spot in the kitchen. Flo still carried a mortgage on her half of the old one-storey building and was struggling to make ends meet.

"The only reason I'm busy is that my prices for food and beer are low, but that also limits my profits. All I can afford is a part-time assistant so the turnover of waitresses is staggering. It's rare for a girl to stay six months before something better comes along. I'm only fifty-seven even though I look at least seventy. Running a diner is all I know, so just like my late Harry, I'll be working here until I drop. On Sundays I close the place at eight. Will you be staying on the couch tonight?"

"Yes, if that's acceptable Flo, but I'll need to continue on my journey in a day or two. Maybe you'll be able to find me a ride south. I don't have enough money to take the bus."

"I look forward to hearing your story later when we get a chance to chat this evening. I should be able to find someone who'll take you on the next leg of your trip."

The day and evening passed quickly and when the last of the customers had left at eight o'clock, Flo exclaimed, "Kate, I couldn't have survived today without you. It's incredible how fast you learned. Now, let's go into the apartment, grab ourselves some beer, and you can tell me all about yourself. You're the most sophisticated homeless person I've ever met and I'm dying to know what's happened to you."

As they got themselves comfortable in the tiny living-room, Sonia decided that she had to tell someone the truth or she'd explode.

"Well Flo, first I'll give you the story I've been using with the folks who've given me rides and asked about my situation. I've claimed that I'm on the run from an abusive, controlling and insane husband. I guess that's what most people expect to hear from a woman my age who's bumming rides."

"I understand, but what's the real story."

"It's so incredibly bizarre that you're probably going to think that I'm at best delusional or at worst, completely crazy. I'm going to leave some things out, like my real name, where I'm from and exactly where I'm going. For you to even come close to knowing what I'm going through, I've got to tell you something about my life before it took a detour into the realm of pure science fiction."

Sonia proceeded to tell Flo about her career, rising to vice-president in a mid-sized company, her two daughters, her bitter divorce and finally meeting Ron about six weeks earlier.

She explained about Ron's amnesia, their budding romance and the wonderful driving trip they took. Eventually Sonia got to the helicopter scare in which Ron bumped his head, and the strange shared dreams and dual personalities which emanated thereafter.

Next came the part about her father's stroke and Sonia's immediate airline flight to reach her Dad's bedside.

"I was frantic that neither of Ron's personalities had called me about the progress of their long drive back to meet me, and at the same time my poor father wasn't recuperating. Mom and I realized that he wasn't going to make it, and Dad passed away last Friday afternoon. I still hadn't heard anything from New or Old Ron, and that's when the story diverts into the truly bizarre. Flo, if you've heard enough, just tell me. You're not going to believe the next part of my story anyway."

"Are you kidding? It's already the most fascinating romance I've ever heard. Continue and you let me decide what I think about the rest of it."

Sonia hesitated for a moment and then launched into the dream in which Cecil appeared and warned her about the creatures, the two parallel worlds, and that to escape she had to transfer from her former world into this one and hope to meet up with Ron.

"I was skeptical, Flo, thinking it was just a strange dream brought on by stress and grief. Just in case it was real, I packed the little bag I've got with me now and went in the middle of the night to the spot where Dad had instructed me to go."

Sonia went on to describe how the hotel did in fact sport a different name after the wave of energy knocked her over. In this alternate reality, she'd cleverly found rides to get as far away as she could from her former home. The most recent ride got her as far as Durant.

"Are you saying that you left everything behind, your Mom, your daughters and grandchildren?"

"That's right. I did mail my mother a note, but since I knew my family would never believe the truth, I just said that Ron was in trouble with dangerous people and that he and I had to go underground for what might be years. In this world I was murdered by one of the creatures last December, apparently because I was randomly chosen as the guinea pig in some awful experiment to determine how the two worlds would differ after just one person was removed from the equation in one of the worlds."

"What will you do if Ron didn't escape?"

"I'll wait around in the spot where we're supposed to meet. At some point I guess I'll have to give up if Ron doesn't show. I haven't even thought about what I'll do in that event. I'm afraid to use my real identity and I have no idea how I'll be able to work for any length of time. I'll be like an illegal alien in my own country, at least sort of my own country except in a parallel world. I can't contact my family here without putting them and myself at risk. I've only been in this reality for about forty-five hours and haven't had time to formulate any contingency plan. If I find Ron, then life will be tolerable since we'll have each other, but if he didn't escape the creatures, then my life is going to be miserable. The only advice that Dad gave me in the dream was to try and create as many changes as possible in this world. Apparently doing so will somehow cause the creatures to lose their ability to control or manipulate either world."

"God, I need another beer," Flo exclaimed. "Can I get you one?"

Sonia nodded but was dying to know what her new friend thought about the story.

"Look Flo, give me your honest reaction. What do you think after hearing what I've told you?"

"It's just too much to take in. I want to believe you, and it's clear that you believe it all, but it's just too farfetched for me to accept. I'm sorry, Kate."

"I can't blame you. From now on I think I'll stick with the abusive husband story. Thanks for listening. I just felt that I needed to get it all off my chest. I'm not crazy, Flo. You don't need to put a chair up against the bedroom door."

"Crazy or not, I like you just fine, Kate. You've been a tremendous help and you're welcome to stay as long as you want. Where is it that you'll be headed after you leave here?"

"I think it's safer for everyone if I don't disclose my exact destination. I'll just say Mexico. Maybe on the morning I leave, you can find someone who's heading south and is willing to have me tag along."

By now it was almost midnight and the ladies decided to call it a night and go to bed.

Sonia had bad dreams in the night but they were too fuzzy to remember much in the morning.

Monday was just as busy with the breakfast rush and at lunchtime, but the supper crowd was thin. Only a few patrons drank that evening.

It was still after one o'clock when Sonia and Flo were finally able to go to bed. Sonia decided that she'd better continue on to San Antonio on Tuesday morning, and informed Flo that she'd be leaving after the breakfast rush.

When Sonia entered the restaurant just after six o'clock on Tuesday morning, Flo tried to insist on paying her for the hours she'd worked.

"Thank you so much Flo, but you gave me a place to sleep and fed me in my time of need. I couldn't possibly accept any money. It's me who owes you an enormous debt of gratitude. If you can find me a ride this morning so that I can continue on my journey, that's more than I could ever have hoped for."

For the next couple of hours, Flo asked each patron where they were headed today. Finally a middle-aged man replied that he was driving to Austin on business. Flo persuaded the gentleman to take her waitress along.

Flo packed some sandwiches for Sonia, hugged her and wished her good fortune in finding Ron and living happily and safely with him.

The driver was very shy and quiet. For most of the journey they just listened to the radio, occasionally making small talk. It was half past two when the man dropped Sonia off at the bus station.

Sonia was pleased to discover that the fare to San Antonio was only $40 and that the next bus departed in less than an hour. She purchased a ticket and at six o'clock Sonia was in San Antonio walking toward the Riverwalk and praying that Ron would be there waiting for her.

CHAPTER 15 (Reunion)

I checked out of my motel at half past ten
on Tuesday morning and walked to the
Riverwalk.

After a quick look around for Sonia, I went
to the hotel overlooking the canal and picked
up my key. The same young desk clerk was on
duty.

It concerned me that Sonia couldn't
possibly recognize me, and I fervently hoped
that her disguise wasn't as impenetrable as
mine.

The Riverwalk area was quite winding and
extensive, and I spent the entire afternoon
walking around or sitting on benches trying to
spot Sonia. It was uncomfortably hot wearing
my money belt covered by the bandages under my
shirt, but I couldn't risk leaving my new life
savings in the hotel room.

I grabbed a hamburger and fries at an
outdoor café for supper, keeping my eyes
peeled.

My watch showed exactly seven o'clock when
my eyes landed on a woman carrying a large
canvas bag while wearing sunglasses and a
scarf on her head. At least a dozen times
since I began scouring the Riverwalk, someone
caught my eye who might be Sonia, but all of
those sightings had turned out to be false
alarms.

I stood up and approached the area where
the woman was leaning against a railing
watching the pretty canal.

When I got a closer look at her, my heart
leapt. My beloved Sonia had eluded Jarlon and
had understood my message.

I walked right up beside the lady, pretended to look away in the distance, and said aloud, "My disguise is better than yours."

Sonia gasped and stammered, "Oh Ron, thank God you made it."

Still gazing out over the canal, I whispered, "Just in case anyone here is looking out for the two of us, I'm staying at the Chez Antoine Hotel in Room 202 about two minutes away. I'll leave first and you can follow me in a moment or so. You can't imagine how relieved I am to see you."

I casually sauntered away and made my way slowly to the lobby of my hotel where I waited. When Sonia entered, I beckoned her to go up the stairway and then followed her.

Once we were safely inside the room, I took off my disguise and we clung to each other for dear life, both of us bathing in a silent joy.

Finally Sonia blurted out, "Ron, what's happened?"

"I doubt if we'll ever fully understand, sweetie. Tell me exactly what you can remember from the moment you flew back to Chicago."

For the next while, we took turns describing what had transpired in each of our lives after we waved goodbye at McCarran International Airport in Las Vegas. We had agreed to listen and not ask questions until we had both finished.

When we were eventually up-to-date on the specific events in our lives, Sonia set the schedule for our attempt at comprehending the situation and asked me to question her experience first before we tackled what had happened to me.

I decided to zero in on the changes I'd noticed between the two worlds.

"Cecil told me in the dreams that his comprehension of the creatures' experiment was that Jarlon eliminated just you from this world we're in now. Have you got any possible explanation why your absence would cause the Rushmore Arms to change its name to Hotel Maximus?"

Sonia contemplated the question for a few moments until a light went off in her brain.

"There is one possibility. I was called out of retirement briefly this past December by the title company where I'd worked. They wanted me to evaluate a complicated financing deal from a title insurer's perspective. The hotel was named the McMillan Ritz at the time and a casino was trying to purchase the hotel from the bankruptcy trustee. I pored over the corporate asset details for a full week and discovered that there was a strange title defect on the Las Vegas Hotel/Casino property that the company intended to use as the main security for its financing. Sections of the land underneath the Las Vegas hotel were actually owned by a private party, not by the company itself, and those sections were also encumbered by two mortgages. I recommended against issuing the title insurance policy and that purchase fell through. The trustee subsequently sold the McMillan Ritz to another purchaser who named the place the Rushmore Arms."

"What would have happened if you had died on December 12th?"

"I don't know. By that date I hadn't completed my evaluation. Without my recommendation to decline coverage, my former employer might well have issued the title policy. A different buyer would certainly have selected another name for its newly purchased hotel."

"That would explain how your death resulted in the same hotel being called different names in each world. The only major changes I've noticed between the two worlds are my existence in the other world but not this one, your absence solely in this world, and the hotel name change. Everything else I saw seemed physically the same."

"The hotel name and the shrubbery around the hotel service entrance were the only differences I noticed," Sonia replied.

"Wait a minute," I interjected. "I did see some other minor discrepancies. There was new furniture in our room at the El Cortez and the hotel lobby had been spruced up. A cash machine had been moved as well. How could that possibly be connected to you?"

"I can make an educated guess," Sonia answered after pondering the question for a moment. "It was the company that owned the El Cortez that lost out on the purchase of the McMillan Ritz, so maybe they decided to redecorate their Las Vegas property instead."

"I guess that's a reasonable theory. That would mean that the changes both in Chicago and Las Vegas can be attributed solely to your absence. Cecil said that I wasn't supposed to have existed in either world. Old Ron should have succumbed to his injuries in both realities. Cecil added that my popping out of the coma in the other world was an anomaly that the creatures didn't anticipate and couldn't comprehend. The aliens only discovered my existence when Old Ron died in this world. That's when Jarlon decided to enter this world and assassinate me. I don't think that I've been responsible for any of the changes between the two worlds."

"You couldn't be more wrong, darling. You've caused enormous differences since you emerged from the coma. There's the lawsuit, the gifts to Liz Cotter and Carl Kaufmann, meeting me, all the travelling we did, not to mention the Cadillac. I wonder where it is in this world right now, maybe still on the dealer's lot in Laughlin. It's probably still languishing in the El Cortez parking garage in our old realm."

"What exactly are you saying?"

"I think it's you who has upended the creatures' controlled experiment, not me. Dad told me in our dream the same thing you told me earlier, that the extent of the changes baffled the creatures. He also said that it was crucial that we create as many additional changes as possible. Somehow by doing so, the creatures' ability to interfere in either world will be diminished or even eliminated. What should we do?"

"We're both exhausted. Let's have a great sleep first and plot our strategy tomorrow when we're fresh. I'm too tired to think straight."

"So am I," Sonia agreed. "I'm going to evaluate what you told me. Tomorrow I'll probably have a ton of questions."

Sonia and I made passionate, desperate love before we fell asleep in each other's arms.

Despite overwhelming odds, we had reunited!

CHAPTER 16 (A Strategy)

We lay in bed on Wednesday morning, hand in hand, while we evaluated our current situation.

I've got less than a hundred dollars to my name," Sonia sighed. "How are you fixed for money?"

"I'm in moderately good shape. I had about $7,000 left over from our trip and so far it's only cost me about $1,000 for buses and hotels. I absconded with well over $30,000 from Old Ron's bank accounts while I was in Laughlin before he died."

"You're kidding," Sonia retorted. "I'm shocked."

"It's kind of my money anyway. That's not all I did. The old boy had never updated his Will but he did leave a note to himself about what he was thinking of doing. I wrote out a handwritten Will for him and took it to a lawyer friend of his after Old Ron died."

I proceeded to tell Sonia which beneficiaries I chose based on Old Ron's statement of intentions.

Sonia concurred that I had done the right thing in the circumstances.

We got up, showered and put on our disguises.

"I've paid for this hotel room for another two nights. We have no idea how proficient the creatures might be in tracking us, but as far as I'm concerned, if Jarlon is already in San Antonio, then we're doomed. I suggest that we continue to wear our disguises but move around normally. Grabbing a nice breakfast seems like a good way to start our new life together."

112

Sonia was amenable so we walked outside on another beautiful sunny day and found a nearby restaurant.

"Where do you think we'll live?" she asked after we had placed our orders.

"I'm open to suggestions. I've got no ties to anything except you. My gut feeling is that Chicago and Laughlin might be too dangerous, and probably Las Vegas as well. In fact we should probably strike off the list of potential residences any place we visited during our driving trip including here in San Antonio. Do you have any strong preferences?"

"I'm not sure. How long do you think we'll have to stay underground until it's safe to emerge from hiding? At some point I'm going to insist on contacting my family."

"I don't have any hard and fast opinion right now, but I expect we should lay low for at least a few months. A lot might depend on how long our money holds out. As much as it pains me to say this, we'll have to live a lot like Old Ron, counting our pennies and wasting nothing."

"How are we going to get around?" Sonia queried. "Relying on buses is both expensive and restricting."

"That's a good point. Maybe today or tomorrow we can try to find a cheap car."

After breakfast we purchased a newspaper and picked up a free community paper on the way back to our hotel. The San Antonio paper didn't have any ads that suited us. Presumably the cost of a classified advertisement was too steep to justify attempting to sell a cheap clunker.

The community paper did have several possibilities, and Sonia spotted three separate ads for cars under $1,000 that all had the same contact telephone number.

I phoned the number and the gentleman who answered barked, "Al's Towing" in a gruff voice.

"I'm looking to purchase an inexpensive automobile and notice that you have three advertised in the community paper. Are they still available?"

The man answered in the affirmative and provided his business address. I said that we'd be around in an hour to take a look at the cars.

It took us forty minutes of brisk walking to find the place, and the owner had "crook" written all over him. He showed us what he had for sale but it was obvious that most of the nicer automobiles had been in a car wreck and tarted up for resale.

The three cheap cars he was trying to flog had each been given a fresh coat of paint but likely nothing else. Al assured us that the cars were all in running order and could be driven right off the lot.

It was apparent that his business was floundering because while we sat in his office, he fielded two successive calls from pestering creditors.

Al didn't seem the least bit embarrassed, and when he hung up after the second call, he spat out, "Damn bill collectors are the scum of the earth. Don't the bastards know we're in a nasty recession?"

"Perhaps we can so some business, Al. We are interested in purchasing one of your cars, and we'll pay cash, but we have a bit of a problem that perhaps you can solve for a small additional fee."

Al perked up. "I'm still listening."

"For reasons I won't get into right now, my wife and I are unable to go to the Department of Motor Vehicles to obtain either a license for the car or a driver's license. We'll be heading far away from here in a day or two and we'll not be returning to your fine state again. We require an unexpired car license as well as the ownership to the vehicle we purchase. In case we're stopped, we need to prove that the car is ours, and the vehicle you sell us has to get us far away from Texas."

"How much is it worth to you if I put a valid license on the car?"

"We'd pay an extra $200, again in cash."

"That ain't much money for the risk I'd be taking."

"On the contrary, the risk to you is virtually zero. We'll soon be out of the state permanently. If you're able to provide us with the ownership without your name appearing anywhere on it, then the car couldn't even be traced back to you."

Al went to a nearby cabinet, pulled out some files and began examining the paperwork.

"Follow me," he ordered as he carried one of the files with him.

We went into a garage on the property. A beat-up and rusted dark green car sat with its hood raised.

"I just towed this crapper in last week. Someone abandoned it on the side of the road when it conked out. I've been able to get it running again but haven't bothered to begin the paperwork to get the ownership transferred into my name. The license sticker on the car doesn't expire until July. It should get you where you want to go, but if it breaks down, that's your problem. You can have it with the license for $800. I'll destroy any records I have about fetching it off the highway, so if I'm ever questioned about it, I'll just say that I know nothing about it."

Sonia and I discussed it in whispered secrecy for a moment. I told Al that we'd accept if the price was dropped to $700. He refused. I thanked him for his time and we stood up to leave.

Realizing that we weren't bluffing, Al relented and we exchanged the cash for the car keys and the ownership.

We drove off, filled our new wheels up with gas and found a municipal parking lot near the Riverwalk that permitted overnight parking. I paid the fee for three days and parked in the rear section of the lot which wasn't visible from the street.

As we walked back to our hotel, I turned to Sonia. "Perhaps we should have asked Al how much it would cost for fake ID. He might have been a one-stop shopping center for all things illegal."

"It's wiser not to buy all our tainted eggs from the same basket," Sonia answered with a mischievous grin.

"I'm uneasy carrying around all this cash but at the moment we don't have any choice. Hopefully when we locate somewhere safe to live, we can find a safe place to stash most of the cash."

Back in our hotel room, we pulled out what maps we had and began to formulate a destination and a route to get there.

"What are your initial thoughts about what to do, Sonia? Should we just travel around or is it better to choose now where we want to live and rent something?"

"It's already getting too hot and humid for my liking this far south. I'm used to a more northerly climate, so my preference would be to head north."

We studied the maps for the rest of the afternoon and again after supper.

"It's a crap shoot trying to pick a city just from its location on a map," I complained. "Let's find an internet café tomorrow and check out websites. That might help us find a place where rentals are cheap and plentiful."

On Thursday morning we found a coffee house with computer access and we surfed the internet for potential places to live in relative obscurity.

While we were on the computer, Sonia announced that she wanted to live either in Illinois or one of the northern states bordering it.

We discussed the options and settled tentatively on either Clinton, Iowa or Monroe, Wisconsin. That decision having been made, we agreed to begin our journey tomorrow morning.

Depending on the reliability of our vehicle, we hoped to travel three or four hundred miles each day.

CHAPTER 17 (On the Road Again)

On Friday morning, since Sonia and I were in no particular hurry and wanted to avoid the morning commuter rush, we had a leisurely breakfast before checking out of our hotel.

We walked to our car, a 2001 Dodge Neon and began our northward-bound journey just after ten o'clock on another gorgeous sunny morning.

We opted for smaller Highway 281 in order to make it a prettier drive. Touring through the towns and villages made for a much more enjoyable experience than would be found sticking to the interstates.

In case the old clunker broke down, we decided that it would be safer and easier to avoid detection on a local highway rather than on a superhighway.

Our goal today was to reach Oklahoma since we deemed it expedient to get out of Texas quickly given the questionable state of our car license plate and ownership.

Our thinking was that if we were stopped by the police for some reason, it would be more difficult for out-of-state cops to ascertain that we weren't the rightful owners of the vehicle registered with Texas license plates.

Sonia and I further decided that if we were stopped, I would show Old Ron's Canadian driver's license. Presumably there would be no need for the police to check its validity.

It was a rather tiring drive but the car held up well and we got a room in a small privately-owned motel just north of Lawton, Oklahoma. We had picked up submarine sandwiches in Lawton when we stopped for gas, and we ate our food in the motel room.

On Saturday we continued on the same highway until we hit the extreme northern part of Kansas at which point we veered east and got a motel in the tiny village of Belleville.

The car had started running a bit rough for the final fifty miles. When we gassed up in Belleville, the attendant checked the oil and found that it was down more than two quarts. I hoped that topping up the oil would fix the engine problem.

Our Sunday drive turned out to be quite worrisome. We had travelled east on Highway 36 into Missouri when the Dodge began to act up again, running noisily and starting to overheat.

I pulled off into a small picnic area and checked the oil which was already very low again. I'd already purchased a six-pack of motor oil at a Wal-Mart we passed in St. Joseph so I was able to replenish the lost oil.

The car still ran noisily as we headed north to Iowa. I had to keep the speed below fifty miles an hour while at the same time running the car heater at full blast on a very hot day. It made for a very uncomfortable ride but that was the only way to keep the little clunker from continuing to overheat.

As a result we couldn't travel as far as we'd planned and took a motel room in Mt. Pleasant, Iowa. We were still about fifty miles from Clinton, the nearest city on our short list of possible places to live.

On Monday I nursed the car to Clinton. We parked downtown and checked the local newspaper for rentals. There were no furnished homes or apartments advertised and very few unfurnished units.

We wandered into a real estate office. The salesperson we spoke with indicated that the home rental market was extremely limited. The only house they had available was a luxury mansion for $3,000 per month.

Sonia and I ate lunch at a diner and discussed our options.

"That luxury rental is out the question," Sonia moaned. "Not only is it far too expensive, but I'm sure they'd want verified financial information and references. The handful of unfurnished apartments advertised in the paper all required one-year leases, so they'd also want confirmation of our circumstances."

"The city's website didn't indicate any housing shortage," I complained. "Monroe is only about seventy-five miles away. I'm thinking we should leave Clinton and check out Monroe."

Back into the hot car we climbed. We crossed the Mississippi River into Illinois and took a series of small highways until we hit Wisconsin.

Monroe was in a somewhat isolated section of southern Wisconsin but we found a decent-looking private motel and took a room for the night.

"This feels like a good place to hide," Sonia opined. "The houses are quite small and the city doesn't seem very prosperous. I noticed quite a few 'FOR SALE' signs and some of those indicated that they were foreclosure sales."

"Rather than approaching a realtor this time," I said, "let's check the newspaper first and then go driving around in order to get a feel for the place."

The classified ads in the local paper showed a much better selection of rentals in this small city of about 10,000 although few apartments were furnished.

We drove around before supper and Sonia spotted a small private "HOUSE FOR RENT" sign at the edge of a driveway.

We couldn't see the actual house from the gravel road, so we drove down the winding dirt lane and came upon a small wooden house with a detached one-car garage. We knocked on the door but it was obvious that no one lived here. Peeking in the window, Sonia exclaimed "It's furnished. This might be perfect for us."

We turned the car around and jotted down the telephone number on the homemade rental sign. When we got back to our motel, Sonia phoned and spoke with a gentleman who agreed to show us the place after supper.

We ate at a restaurant near our motel and plotted out our strategy.

"I think now's the time to get rid of my disguise," I said. "No one is going to want to rent a house to a long-haired bearded hippie. The realtor back in Clinton didn't even want to shake my hand."

"What about me?" Sonia asked. "It's possible that someone from Chicago will come along and recognize me."

"Since you're dead in this world, I think all you need to do is keep wearing the glasses and maybe adopt a different hairstyle. The scarf is also effective as a disguise, but I'll leave it entirely up to you. People around here will think that you're either weird or dying of cancer if you never go outside without a scarf around your head. It should be safe ditching our disguises. They were effective in getting us safely out of harm's way. I'm sure that the creatures could never follow our tracks."

We kept our disguises on until we were approaching the rental home at which point we removed them.

I introduced us as Ron and Sonia Smith.

The landlord was Ted Perlberg and he explained as he showed us the house that it was his mother's home but that she had passed away in March.

"Title's all buggered up right now and it's going to take a while to get things straightened up, but the bills keep coming in and I'm falling behind."

"This might work out perfectly for both of us," I said amicably. "My wife and I just arrived from Texas and we want to try living in this area first before we decide whether to sell our home in Texas and move our belongings up here. Fortunately for us, our son is in between wives at the moment and he's looking after our home down there. How much is the rent?"

"I was hoping to fetch six hundred a month plus maybe another hundred to cover the heat and hydro."

"That's certainly well within our budget if it includes most of the furniture. When you're successful in getting the title cleared up, how quickly would you need us to vacate?"

"I hadn't thought about it. Does one month sound reasonable?"

"That would be fine. The place is a bit overgrown at the moment. Would you mind if Sonia and I spruced it up a bit? We're both retired and like to putter around outdoors."

"Of course I wouldn't mind. It would make the place easier for me to sell. If we come to an agreement, when would you like to move in?"

"Since we're in a motel tonight, we'd be amenable to paying you now and moving in tomorrow, assuming that would give you enough time to remove your mother's personal items. We haven't had an opportunity to open bank accounts so we'll have to pay you in cash."

"If we keep everything under the table," Ted suggested, "then the IRS doesn't need to know anything about our arrangement. That means I can't give you a receipt. I already took all of Mom's personal stuff out of here so nobody could steal anything valuable. I can give you the keys now if you pay me the rent."

"That's perfectly acceptable, Ted. There's a bit more than a week left in May. Why don't we pay you $200 for the rest of May and $700 for the month of June?"

And that was that. Sonia and I now had a place to call home. We were quite pleased as we drove back to the motel, again with each of us wearing our disguises.

CHAPTER 18 (Stirring Things Up)

After breakfast on Tuesday we checked out of the motel and drove to our new digs where we took off our disguises for good. The house was in the country about a quarter mile from the east end of Monroe.

There was a small shopping plaza with a grocery store within reasonable walking distance but we stopped there and loaded up the car with groceries, beer and wine. We decided to put our car in the garage and use it only for emergencies.

Later in the day we walked back into town and spotted a yard sale where we purchased two used bicycles with the old-fashioned metal basket carriers attached to the handlebars.

Sonia and I had discussed our strategy and concluded that we had a duty to mankind to cause as many differences as possible in Monroe, hoping that by doing so, the creatures would lose all control over the two parallel worlds and Sonia and I would no longer be in any danger.

As the weeks passed, we joined a church and got involved in various community-oriented projects.

My sixty-fifth birthday arrived on July 26th and we celebrated by sharing a lovely dinner at a fancy restaurant in Monroe.

Ted Perlberg got his property title issues cleared up in the fall, but he was happy to have us continue to rent the house since it was providing him with a tax-free income. Ted was an auto mechanic and we had him repair our old Dodge so that it would be more reliable if we needed it again. Except when Ted drove it around the neighborhood once or twice to determine if his repairs had been successful, the little beast remained hidden in the garage.

One Friday evening in early October as Sonia and I were drinking wine after a lovely home-cooked supper, she asked whether I felt that enough time had elapsed to permit her to make contact with her family.

"There's no way of knowing for sure, honey. Don't forget, it's not really your family. Approaching them would cause tremendous confusion and possibly even put their lives in danger. If Jarlon is somehow monitoring their lives waiting for you to reach out to them, there's no telling what some alien with no compassion or morals would be capable of doing."

"But we've been helping out in the church and in the community to make a positive difference in people's lives. Surely we've caused enough changes by now that the creatures have lost control."

Just then another political advertisement on TV blared out and interrupted our train of thought.

"It's strange," I whined. "These politicians are slamming each other as if next year's election is the most crucial matter facing America, and yet we're living underground to escape aliens which have the power to step in and exterminate whomever they choose."

"If in fact we've been successful in severing the ability of the creatures to affect the two parallel worlds Ron, then this election is just as important as the candidates believe. Somebody needs to get America's finances back to sanity before it's too late. Getting back to my question, is it too soon to contact Mom and the girls?"

"I'll acquiesce to whatever you decide, darling, but my gut is telling me that it's prudent to wait a bit longer."

Sonia hesitated, deep in thought, and then proclaimed, "There must be ways that we can multiply the effects of the two of us being alive in this reality where we're not supposed to exist. What else can we do to really stir things up?"

"I'm not running for President, if that's what you're proposing," I joked.

"I'm serious, Ron. How can we influence more people?"

"I guess we could launch some sort of letter writing campaign," I answered, "but what would we say and who would believe us?"

"Maybe we could provide our identities to the authorities and let them verify that we both died in this world," Sonia suggested.

"That's a possibility, but it could back-fire big time. The police would probably conclude that we're either con artists or nut jobs, and Jarlon would discover our whereabouts."

"I think I've got a better idea, Ron. We could write a book about our experiences and publish it anonymously without disclosing where we live."

"Now that's thinking outside the box, sweetie. At the very least, the book will be out there disclosing the truth even if it gets classified as fiction. Presumably the more folks who read it, the more changes in this world the book might cause."

"Actually there should be two separate books," Sonia exclaimed. "The first one will be about our lives in the other world up to the point at which you and Old Ron had your dream fight. The second book will chronicle each of our lives beginning just before we were transported into this parallel world."

"That's a tremendous concept, Sonia. We'll need to purchase a couple of computers to make it easier to write the books. We won't hook the computers up to the internet, but once the books are written, then we can download them onto a memory stick and send them to a publisher."

The very next day we checked out used computers in the classified ads and purchased two older desktop models for $100 from a local family who even delivered them to us.

Sonia and I kept ourselves busy and contented with a combination of our community involvement and the writing of the two books.

By the end of December I had completed the first book with Sonia's help, which we decided to call "FRUGAL LAWYER, FLASHY LAWYER." It dealt with Old Ron's experiment with living among the poor, the details of which I recalled from having carefully read Old Ron's diary while I was living in his apartment in both worlds. This book also described Old Ron's mugging, my emergence from the coma and the intense competition between the old boy and me to gain superiority in that world and win Sonia's heart.

Sonia had been working feverishly on putting her own adventures on paper. Each night we would carefully read what the other had written and make notes or suggestions.

Once I'd completed the first book, I was able to begin writing my portion of the sequel about being transported into this parallel world, watching Old Ron die in the hospital and then fleeing for my life after Cecil had warned me about the alien creatures in our shared dreams.

By mid-January we finally completed the joint venture second book. We ended that portion of the story in San Antonio when we decided to live underground for a period of time. Sonia and I both agreed that providing any details of our car purchase and trip back north would be unwise.

We ended the book with a vague epilogue stating that Ron and Sonia had found a safe place to live and that they decided to write the books to warn the world about the alien creatures.

Now we were ready to get both books printed.

Neither of us knew anything about the publishing business but we were convinced that a traditional publisher would laugh at us.

After doing a bit of research using a computer at the library, we discovered the phenomenon of self-publishing. Many businesses had sprung up to permit writers to publish their books as long as they were willing to foot the cost out of their own pockets.

We found a small outfit in Madison which was both friendly and helpful when we contacted it. For a total price of $4,000, the publisher agreed to provide us with one hundred soft-cover copies of each book. That price also included international E-Book registration which meant that our books would automatically be available throughout the world on-line at the major book-selling websites.

Our first and only argument with the company related to how the books would be classified on the book-selling sites. We tried to insist that both books be classified as non-fiction, but the publisher adamantly refused, explaining that the book sellers themselves would individually decide under which classifications they would market our books.

Sonia and I had to accept a compromise solution. An explanatory page was inserted at the beginning of the second book, which was entitled "ALIEN ASSASSINS ARE AFTER US." It read as follows:

The authors claim that the events set forth in this book actually occurred and that they are still on the run in this world from the creatures. Readers can decide for themselves whether to believe this story. The authors strongly recommend that their first published book, "FRUGAL LAWYER, FLASHY LAWYER" be read in order to better understand the background to this second book. The authors are currently hiding in a location unknown to the publisher.

We used our real names as the co-authors of both books. Since the publisher insisted on seeing proper identification, we decided not to put our pictures on the book covers. We used our disguises each time we met the publisher and felt that it would be too confusing to reveal our true appearance to her and useless to put our disguised photos on the covers. If we displayed our actual photos, then our friends and neighbors in Monroe could easily identify us if they happened to see the books.

As it was, the publisher was already uncomfortable with our lack of an internet address or telephone and our use of a post office box in Madison as our only contact address. We were concerned that if we disclosed to the publisher that our appearance was in fact an elaborate disguise, the company might have refused to publish our books.

Fortunately non-photo ID had been sufficient to satisfy the publisher's request to see some form of proper identification.

On Monday, February 15th, 2016 our books were ready to be picked up. Sonia and I were thrilled with them. It would take another week before the books would be available on the internet since they had to be digitally sent to the on-line book-sellers and catalogued.

We purchased boxes of large envelopes and inserted a copy of each book along with a covering letter stating that these stories were the gospel truth. Then we addressed each envelope and mailed our books to newspapers and other media outlets all over North America.

Sonia insisted on sending a copy to her mother and each of her daughters as well as to her ex-husband and her former employer. She included a personalized note in each of those mailings. Then as an afterthought Sonia also sent a copy to Flo in Durant, Oklahoma.

I sent copies to the Laughlin police department to the attention of Detective Peter McCabe, to Laughlin General Hospital as well as to Ben Van Huizen, the lawyer in Belleville who had worked in the same building as Ron, and to Tammy Mick in Sarnia, Liz Cotter, Carl Kaufmann and Peter Long in Laughlin. I wrote a separate note to each of those recipients explaining that the Ronald Smith they knew never had a twin brother. I explained in the note, just as set out in the books, it was a different facet of his personality which emerged from the coma in the other parallel world, a phenomenon that didn't occur in this reality.

The only portion I left out of both the book and my notes to the people in Laughlin was the fact that I had forged Old Ron's Last Will and Testament. As far as I was concerned, it was a non-essential piece of information and would cause severe problems in processing Old Ron's estate. Even if most of the money had been distributed by now, distant relatives of Old Ron or even the government itself might seek to overturn the Will. That would cause immense and unnecessary problems for all of Old Ron's friends.

Our hands were sore as we carted the duly stuffed envelopes the next day to various post offices in South Beloit, Illinois and in Janesville and Madison, Wisconsin.

The postage alone cost more than $500 but we felt satisfied that our stories had been told to as many folks as possible.

Fortunately our old car made the various trips to Madison as well as the final postal run without incident. I had altered the tiny Texas license plate sticker in the upper right corner of the plate from "JUL 15" to "JULY 16" with paint, and I actually did a reasonably credible job of it.

A few days later at an internet café in Monroe, we located our books on the Amazon website and on the sites of some other E-Book publishing companies.

Sonia and I quivered with excitement as we assured each other that everyone on the planet with access to the internet could now obtain a copy of our books.

How's that working out for you, Jarlon? Are your powers slipping away?

CHAPTER 19 (Contacting Family)

Over the ensuing month we concentrated on our community and church work. We attended a large banquet in Monroe in which the volunteers from the many local charities were thanked and treated to a lovely meal.

Much to our chagrin, the food bank volunteers were singled out and we had to pose with the group for a picture. It would have looked suspicious if we refused but we consoled ourselves with the certainty that no one would recognize us in a group shot published in a tiny rural community newspaper.

From time to time we would check the internet websites of the various booksellers but the results based on the ranking of the books was quite disheartening. On Amazon alone, there were millions of books in competition with our own including a staggering number of free offerings.

Our aim of disseminating our story to a wide audience was turning out to be quite futile. Only a very few of our books were purchased by readers and none of them had bothered to post a review indicating what they thought of our strange allegations that alien assassins were scouring this world in search of us.

Although Sonia and I were content and happy together, always in the background was her deep desire to contact her family.

On the morning of March 16th, after stepping out of the shower wrapped only in a towel, Sonia marched into the kitchen where I was having my coffee, and announced, "My mother will be eighty-five next Tuesday, and I need to see her. My mind's made up. Mom won't be around forever and she's had plenty of time to digest our books and discuss them with the girls. How can we contact Mom without putting her and us in danger?"

"Telephoning Bernice certainly didn't work for me last year. Your mother was totally confused, Karen was dismissive and Jeff warned me never to call the family again. I'm sure they believe that the books are total fiction, created by me solely to make money from some sick obsession I have with your family."

"I'm sure you're right. In that case, we'll have to arrange a face to face meeting somehow."

"It's far too risky to just show up at your mother's apartment. If the creatures have been monitoring Bernice and your daughters all this time waiting for you to contact one of them, then we're signing our own death warrants and possibly putting your family in grave danger at the same time."

"Then we'll have to make contact somewhere other than at their homes," Sonia insisted. "Sorry to be so bull-headed, but I won't wait any longer."

"There's no way of knowing when or where your mother goes to get her groceries. Stalking her would make us stick out like sore thumbs and it might take days before Bernice actually went anywhere."

Sonia fell silent and went in to the bedroom to get dressed.

When she returned to the kitchen she was animated.

"Get yourself and your disguise ready, Mr. Smith. We're driving down to Rockford, Illinois. I've had a brainstorm."

Sonia refused to divulge what she had come up with.

It took us an hour and fifteen minutes to reach the western outskirts of Rockford. Sonia directed me to stop at a shopping mall where she found a bank of pay phones at the rear entrance. I stood beside her as she called information and obtained the number of a physician's office. Then she called the number.

"Hello, I'm Bernice Poniecki's granddaughter. Granny thinks she has an appointment with Doctor Peden coming up but she's lost the little reminder card. Can you check your records for me?"

"Of course; I'll just pull her file up. Yes, Bernice was correct. Her appointment is next Wednesday at eleven in the morning. Tell Bernice not to worry. We would have called her the day prior in order to remind her."

"Thank you so much. I'll bring Granny around to see you next Wednesday."

Sonia smirked as she hung up the phone.

"I'm not just a pretty face, Ronald. We're going to Chicago next week."

We surfed the internet while having lunch in a restaurant at the mall. Both of our books had risen slightly in the rankings but it appeared that few new readers had surfaced. We drove back to Monroe without incident.

It was rather disheartening that sending our books to newspapers and other media outlets all over the country had proven to be pointless. Not one single article had been published by any of the media outlets, at least none that we could locate on the internet.

Sonia was both excited and distracted for the next several days, trying to decide

134

exactly what to say to her mother and whichever daughter drove Bernice to the doctor's appointment.

On Wednesday we woke very early and set out for Chicago just before seven. It took us a couple of hours to reach the small two-storey building housing Dr. Phillip Peden's medical practice and various other offices.

There was a small strip mall next door. Deciding to exercise an abundance of caution, we parked in the rear of that plaza in such a way that we could monitor the parking lot for Doctor Peden's building.

I made the first foray inside. Sonia followed a few minutes later.

On the first floor there were three separate offices and two sets of stairs leading up to the second floor, one at the front of the building and the other at the rear leading to the parking lot. There was no elevator.

I ascended the front stairway and checked out what was on the second floor.

Dr. Peden's clinic took up one half of the floor and the remainder housed another doctor's office which was closed on Wednesdays.

There was a small washroom at the end of the hall near the front stairwell. Another door, which I found unlocked, led into a small common waiting area, presumably to accommodate any overflow if both offices were extremely busy on any particular day.

When Sonia arrived I showed her what I had discovered. We discussed a strategy to permit a private visit and decided that the small waiting room was the ideal location.

I returned to the car first and Sonia followed a few minutes later.

At quarter to eleven Sonia gasped as we watched Karen step out of a car and escort Bernice to the rear entrance of the building.

This time Sonia left first and I followed her a few minutes later. While Sonia remained in the small waiting room, I waited in the hallway near Dr. Peden's office.

The door opened twice and patients came out and went down the stairway.

CHAPTER 20 (Family Reunion)

The doctor's office door opened again and Bernice came out first with Karen right behind her.

"Good morning Mrs. Poniecki and Karen," I said cheerily. "There's a belated eighty-fifth birthday surprise waiting for you just down the hall. Please follow me."

"What's this all about?" Karen asked suspiciously. With my long-haired hippie disguise, I certainly didn't resemble anyone who would know Bernice.

"It wouldn't be a surprise if I told you. There's someone in this waiting room who wants to wish Bernice a very happy birthday."

I opened the door, ushered the ladies inside and then closed the door behind me.

Sonia had removed her sunglasses and scarf and slowly turned to face her guests.

A visibly shaken Bernice kept repeating, "I don't understand."

Karen stood there speechless.

"It's really me," Sonia whispered with tears in her eyes. "The books we sent you were true. There really is a parallel world. This is my true love, Ron Smith and we've been hiding from the creatures since last May when both of us were transported from our own world into this one."

I removed my disguise in an attempt to convince the ladies that I wasn't some hippie freak con-man.

"It was me who telephoned you early last May looking for Sonia. As you can see, I eventually found her. Forgive these furtive arrangements, but we really have no idea whether the creatures who want to kill us might still be monitoring your homes and telephones."

"I don't believe this garbage for a minute," Karen snapped.

"It's true, sweetie," Sonia replied gently. "I still have some of my ID from the other world."

Karen examined Sonia's driver's license and birth certificate but remained unconvinced.

Bernice had sat down in one of the chairs and just stared wordlessly at Sonia.

"I wasn't expecting this level of skepticism," Sonia moaned. "The two worlds were apparently identical until the creatures decided to exterminate me in this world. Ask me anything that happened before I died here, things that only I could possibly know."

"Do you know a Canadian woman named Jane Holland?" Bernice asked.

"No. Who is she?"

"A woman phoned me recently asking about you and the books."

"You never mentioned that call to me, Gran," Karen exclaimed.

For the next ten minutes both Karen and Bernice threw questions at Sonia. By the end of the interrogation, both women were fully convinced.

For another thirty minutes Sonia grilled them about the grandchildren and a myriad of other family matters, seemingly fascinated by any events that had occurred in the past year.

I put my disguise back on and said I'd wait for Sonia in the car. I assured her that she could take all the time she wanted to visit her family.

Both Bernice and Karen hugged me just before I left the room.

It was another two hours before I saw Bernice and Karen exit the building. Five minutes later an emotional Sonia opened the car door.

As we began driving back to Monroe, Sonia's verbal floodgates poured open as she tried to describe the emotions that this secret visit had unleashed.

"Mom and Karen tried to imagine how they would have been affected by my note to them in the other world that I was running away with you and hiding underground for an indefinite period. They both agreed that although they'd be worried sick, it would be a thousand times better than what they actually went through in this world when I was murdered."

"I'm so pleased for you, darling. Your visit turned out to a complete success. Did you tell them where we're living?"

"Yes, but they promised not to tell anyone, especially Nancy. Karen is going to tell Jeff about today's visit but we both agreed that it's too much for Nancy or any of the grandchildren to grasp. Nancy is the emotional one in our family whereas Karen has always been like me, rational and analytical. Apparently Nancy was extremely upset and angry when she read our books. Once the coast is clear and any danger from the creatures has passed, then you and I can come back to Chicago and start living a normal life."

"Have you made any tentative arrangements for another visit?"

"We haven't made any specific plans, but Karen gave me the phone number of the exercise room at her health club, and she'll make a point of being there every Sunday afternoon at two o'clock. That provides an untraceable opportunity for me to contact her if necessary. I told her that I'd only call if something important came up since we only make phone calls from another city in order to avoid detection."

Sonia continued talking excitedly all the way back home. I was relieved that the visit had been a rousing success and completely undetectable.

Perhaps Sonia and I were too clever for the creatures to have any realistic chance of finding us. They weren't so all-powerful after all.

CHAPTER 21 (An Inquisitive Reader)

Jane Holland finished the last chapter of the book "ALIEN ASSASSINS ARE AFTER US" and put her Kindle E-Reader down on the bed beside her.

What a fascinating story!

The writers certainly had active imaginations. Jane was pleased that she had selected this particular book on Amazon based solely on the unusual title and a bizarre statement in the descriptive blurb indicating that the authors claimed that the whole story was true. Jane loved good science fiction and the authors' concepts in this novel had been fascinating.

She picked her E-Reader back up and scrolled to the "About the Author" page. Unlike every other book she had ever read, this one contained no biographical data whatsoever, only their names.

Jane got on her computer and called up Amazon's product page for the novel. The brief description designed to attract potential purchasers was short and merely said, "Imagine another world out there, identical to this one. Both worlds are observed by heartless creatures who concoct a cruel experiment. They murder one woman, Sonia Poniecki in just one of the worlds for the sole purpose of following the tiny subsequent changes that the absence of that one solitary person would cause. Against all logic, the changes between the two worlds escalate exponentially. The creatures decide to murder the same woman in the other world in order to stop those inexplicable changes. What follows is a tale of adventure and terror as Sonia desperately attempts to elude these alien assassins. The authors claim that the story is actually true."

Jane went back on her E-Reader and read again the book's introduction page. It recommended an earlier book entitled "FRUGAL LAWYER, FLASHY LAWYER" in order for readers to understand how Ron and Sonia first met.

Jane found the earlier book on Amazon's website and purchased it. Within a few minutes she had successfully downloaded it onto her E-Reader.

Glancing at her clock, it was only quarter past ten, so Jane decided to read a few pages before turning the lights out.

Three hours later she reached the final page. This prequel was actually a combination of romance and humor with no science fiction element whatsoever.

Coincidentally, Ronald Smith had operated his legal practice right here in the city of Belleville. It intrigued Jane that a tiny portion of the story related to the city she now called home.

Jane tried to reconcile what she remembered about the characters in the second book with what she had just learned about them in this first segment.

Again there was no biographical information contained in the E-Book or on the Amazon book information page. Instead there was a sentence directing readers to the sequel "ALIEN ASSASSINS ARE AFTER US" in order to learn the fate of Ron and Sonia.

Pleased that she had discovered a new favorite author, Jane went to sleep basking in the unique enjoyment that only a good book could provide.

The next morning Jane found herself mesmerized by the mystery surrounding the two authors.

Both books were copyrighted in 2016. Jane went back on the Amazon website and pulled up both books, each of which showed a release date of February 17, 2016. Since it was only February 23rd today, that meant that the books had only been on the market for a week.

Jane noted that the publisher was an outfit in Madison, Wisconsin. On checking out its web page, Jane discovered that it was a self-publishing company which meant that the authors had paid to publish the books out of their own pockets. Perhaps that explained why the authors had used their own names for the main characters. They were novices and didn't know any better.

Immensely curious about the authors, Jane phoned the publisher and spoke with a very pleasant lady, Helen Kirkwood who had dealt directly with Ronald Smith and Sonia Poniecki. Helen was quite forthcoming and disclosed that she had indeed met both authors but that they were extremely secretive and alleged that the books described actual events, not fictional ones.

Jane did elicit a post office box address for the authors after she mentioned to Ms. Kirkwood that she wanted to send a congratulatory letter to the authors.

Fully expecting to find that the names used in the books were entirely fictitious, Jane googled "Ronald Smith + Laughlin Ontario" and was astounded to discover newspaper articles describing his mugging and coma. A final brief piece confirmed Ron's death months later. The obituaries in the Laughlin Tribune didn't include one for Ronald Smith but a further search of the official Province of Ontario death records did elicit that Ronald Ward Smith had in fact died in Laughlin, Ontario on May 14th, 2015.

It was clear that portions of the first book remarkably mirrored real events.

Jane took a break to phone her mother. She described the interesting books she had read the previous day and mentioned that she was now trying to debunk or verify the story by searching items on the internet.

"I'm sure if anyone can ferret out the truth, it's you," Silvia joked. "When it comes to solving any mystery, you've always been like a dog with a bone, even when you were a little girl."

After half an hour of chat, Jane made herself a sandwich and got back on the computer.

This time she searched "Sonia Poniecki + Chicago" and was even more puzzled when both a newspaper article about the woman's murder and her obituary popped up, each containing a clear picture. It was eerie that even the names of Sonia's next-of-kin correlated precisely with the details in the books."

Jane printed off the materials and adjourned to her living-room to evaluate what she'd discovered.

After thirty minutes of contemplation, Jane decided that she was sufficiently intrigued to take the investigation to the next level, which would entail rereading both books carefully and making copious notes regarding dates, characters and anything else that was verifiable.

That task took the remainder of Saturday and all Sunday morning and afternoon.

After supper Jane got back on her computer. With her notebooks and charts beside her, Jane began fact checking.

She found and downloaded a picture from Ronald Smith's retirement notice in the Belleville Intelligencer, and Jane now felt that she was beginning to know the characters. Somehow putting faces to the names was comforting.

The following morning Jane forwarded the pictures to Helen Kirkwood by email and asked the publisher to confirm whether the authors she had met matched the photos of the deceased.

Within an hour Helen had replied that the Ronald Smith she met had long hair and a beard but that Sonia Poniecki was somewhat similar in appearance to the newspaper photos, although the author had worn sunglasses and a head scarf each time she attended at the publishing company. Helen indicated that she was also becoming fascinated with these mysterious authors, and requested that Jane provide additional information as she discovered it.

Jane studied her notes and the chronology of the stories. She spent an hour trying to track down a diner in downtown Durant, Oklahoma operated by a woman named Flo. The internet searches were fruitless but finally Jane telephoned some restaurants in that small city that did have websites, and discovered that the person she was seeking was Florence Clarke who owned a place named "Harry's Diner and Bar."

Jane obtained the phone number and called. Flo herself answered but was too busy with customers to talk and suggested that Jane call again at three o'clock when the diner wasn't so busy.

When she did call back, Flo confirmed that a woman calling herself Kate had shown up last May. Flo surprised Jane by revealing that she had recently received the two books in the mail along with a brief letter indicating that Kate was in fact Sonia Poniecki, and that she had found Ron in San Antonio, but that they were still hiding from the creatures.

"What did you think when you read the books?" Jane asked.

"I haven't had a chance to read them yet. I work eighteen hour days. I looked at the covers but just put the books back in the envelope. It's been twenty years since I've read a book. Kate told me all about the aliens anyway when she stayed at my place. I didn't believe her."

"If I email Sonia's picture to you, would you confirm if it's the same person you met as Kate?"

"I guess so, but I don't own a computer."

With a bit of prodding, Flo agreed to obtain the email address of her nephew. Jane could call back later to get the details and send the pictures. Jane also persuaded Flo to read the few pages of the second book regarding the Durant stopover and to let Jane know from where the envelope had been postmarked.

That evening Jane called back, got the pertinent information and sent the photos to Flo's nephew with a message to print off the pictures and take them to Flo's restaurant.

Flo had checked the envelope and advised that it had been mailed from South Beloit, Illinois.

On Tuesday morning Jane phoned Flo again.

146

"It's kind of spooky," Flo began. "Kate sure looks like the woman who was murdered in Chicago. They must be twins or something."

"Did you get a chance to read the chapter about Durant?"

"Yes, and the book described exactly what actually happened here. Kate wouldn't take any money for the time she worked but I was able to find a customer who would drive her south. He was back in the diner a couple of weeks later and said that he had dropped Kate off in Austin just like the book says. What do you make of the whole thing?"

"I haven't formed any solid conclusions yet, Flo. It might just be an elaborate publicity stunt to sell more books, but I'm having a great time trying to solve the mystery. I'll let you know if I ever discover the truth. Thanks so much for being so helpful."

Feeling that she was making great progress, Jane contacted Ben Van Huizen, the lawyer in Belleville. She introduced herself as a writer preparing a book review of the two books by Ronald Smith, and had a lovely chat in which she learned about the frugal side of Ronald Smith.

Mr. Van Huizen admitted that he had received copies of the books in the mail and had loved the stories. He assumed that Donald Smith, the twin brother who had surfaced out of nowhere, had actually written the books. The lawyer also confirmed that his books had been mailed from Janesville, Wisconsin.

Jane made one final call to Peter Long, the lawyer in Laughlin. He was somewhat more reserved in his response, but he did confirm that he personally met both Ronald Smith and Donald Smith, that they were shockingly identical twins, and that he had recently been sent copies of the two books.

"By any chance did you notice where the books had been mailed from?" Jane asked.

"Yes I did, because I was curious. They were sent from Madison, Wisconsin."

"Did you read the books, Mr. Long?"

"Yes, and they were unusually creative."

"Did you believe any of it?"

"Of course not; in my business I deal in provable facts, not science fiction mumbo jumbo, but that doesn't mean that I didn't thoroughly enjoy the books. I'd never read anything in which my wife, my nephews and myself were all part of the story line."

Jane thanked the attorney for taking the time to speak with her.

That evening Jane debated with herself whether it would be too crass to phone the mother of Sonia Poniecki in Chicago.

When she awoke on Wednesday morning, Jane came to a decision. She would call Sonia's mother but would be extremely tactful in doing so. She obtained Bernice Poniecki's phone number and rang it. An elderly lady answered and confirmed that she was Bernice.

"Hello, Mrs. Poniecki. My name is Jane Holland and I'm calling from Canada. I'm preparing a book review of two recently published novels. The first one is entitled "FRUGAL LAWYER, FLASHY LAWYER" and the second book is "ALIEN ASSASSINS ARE AFTER US." The authors of both books are shown as Ronald Smith and Sonia Poniecki. By any chance have you read those books yet?"

"Oh my, I don't know what to say. Yes, someone sent me the books in the mail and I did read them, but as you know, they are about my late daughter, Sonia. I found them terribly unsettling. My granddaughter and her husband, who also received the books in the post, were livid with anger when they read them."

"Do you have any idea who actually wrote the books, Bernice?"

"Jeff, my son-in-law, is certain that it must be Ron Smith. He's a delusional man who called here last year looking for Sonia, and he claimed to be her boyfriend. Jeff took the call when I became confused and he asked the man not to contact us again and to seek professional therapy. Jeff is a doctor, you know. All the books were mailed to us from South Beloit which is upstate."

"The second book refers to Mr. Smith's telephone call to you," Jane responded. "I found it odd that the book was also so accurate about the details of your family. I read the obituaries for Sonia and for Cecil. The information corresponded exactly to what is set out in the book. I'm an avid reader but I've never read a piece of fiction which contains the names of real people and includes their personal histories."

"Jeff believes that Ron Smith has developed some fixation on Sonia, perhaps from seeing the newspaper articles about her death, and Jeff thinks that Mr. Smith truly believes in his delusion that he is Sonia's boyfriend."

"I take it from what you're telling me that no one in your family believes that either book is true."

"No dear; it's all fantasy flowing out of Ron Smith's troubled mind."

Jane couldn't think of anything else pertinent to ask the poor lady, so she thanked Bernice for being so candid and said goodbye.

Jane called her own mother and related the details of what she'd uncovered over the past few days.

When she got off the phone, Jane pondered whether to accept Bernice Poniecki's explanation or continue to pursue the matter. Jane's naturally inquisitive personality won out.

What harm could come from digging a little deeper?

Besides, it was great fun.

CHAPTER 22 (More Investigating)

After breakfast the next morning, Jane
drove to the local CAA office and picked up
maps of Illinois, Wisconsin, Texas, Oklahoma,
Kansas, Missouri and Iowa.

It was apparent that Ron and Sonia had made
their way at some point since last May from
San Antonio up to Madison, Wisconsin.

They likely now lived somewhere in southern
Wisconsin or northern Illinois, based on their
choices of book publisher and places from
where they had mailed off their books. Since
Helen Kirkwood had met personally with Ron and
Sonia several times during the book publishing
process, they must reside within easy driving
distance of Madison.

All the books were mailed either from
Madison or from locations south of that city.
That would suggest that Ron and Sonia lived
south of Madison.

Jane pored over the maps and chose to focus
on a radius of fifty miles from Janesville,
Wisconsin which was the middle location of the
three cities from which books were sent.

She began surfing the internet looking for
newspapers published within that area, and
made a list of the dozen or so publications
she was able to locate on-line.

Sonia's surname was uncommon so Jane
focused first on her, but found no hits
whatsoever in any of the newspapers.

Ronald Smith was an extremely common name
and there were many references in the various
papers. Jane painstakingly read them all,
rejected most as definitely not her man, and

printed off half a dozen articles that could possibly be the correct Ronald Smith.

Over the next couple of days she attempted to obtain additional information by telephone about each Ronald Smith in the stories, and was reasonably satisfied that none of them was about the man she was tracking.

Beginning to get discouraged, Jane reminded herself that finding Ronald or Sonia in a newspaper article was not very likely. After all, they were trying to remain inconspicuous. Publishing the books was possibly their only venture outside their cave.

Each morning Sonia would recheck the various newspapers on the slim chance that she would hit pay dirt.

On Sunday evening she went to her mother's condominium for supper and was moaning to Silvia about the dead end Jane had encountered.

"Belleville has both a regular newspaper and two free community papers," Silvia mentioned. "Have you been checking the free ones as well as the main publications?"

"No I haven't, and that's a great idea Mom. Tomorrow I'll get back on the computer and see if I can find out what free papers are distributed in my search area."

Other matters filled Jane's time over the next few days so it wasn't until Thursday evening when she sat at her computer and began compiling a list of free community newspapers. It wasn't easy finding them, but by the time she turned off her computer, Jane had found fifteen publications. She had no way of knowing if there were others.

On Friday afternoon Jane spotted a hot prospect in a small free paper called "South Central Wisconsin Community Press." A banquet to honor helpers at local charities contained a photo of food bank volunteers from the small city of Monroe, two of which were identified as Ron and Sonia Smith.

The picture wasn't particularly clear since the group photo contained almost fifty volunteers, but there was a certain similarity in the appearance of Mr. and Mrs. Smith with the pictures Jane had downloaded of the people she was tracking.

The food bank didn't appear to have its own telephone number despite calls Jane made to the Monroe Chamber of Commerce and to the community newspaper itself.

For the next few days Jane tried to learn as much as she could about Monroe, Wisconsin. Over that period she made additional phone calls to various outfits in Monroe and finally obtained the number for the head volunteer of the food bank.

Despite calling each day, no one answered until Sunday evening on March 20th.

The rather elderly lady was very pleasant and Jane had a nice chat with her. Claiming that from the banquet picture Jane thought she recognized Ron and Sonia Smith as old friends, Jane sought a contact telephone number.

The woman seemed anxious to accommodate Jane's request and retrieved the food bank volunteer list.

"I'm so sorry, dear. I don't know this couple personally since I'm a bit too old now to actually put in hours at the distribution center. It appears that they don't have a telephone. Their address on our records is Rural Route 2, Monroe but that's all the information I have about them. I guess you'll have to write to them in order to find out if they really are the folks you know."

Jane thanked the woman for her assistance.

The following morning Jane got on the internet and checked air fares to Chicago. She selected a direct flight out of Toronto, leaving this upcoming Saturday, March 26th and returning on Wednesday, March 30th. Jane also booked a rental car for her time in the USA.

The whole situation was quite exciting, and the thought of combining a vacation with her new hobby as a sleuth buoyed Jane's spirits considerably. She began reminiscing about her time so far in Canada.

Since retiring from her career in the banking industry in England a year earlier and moving back to Canada to be near her mother, Jane had not been able to find a routine that provided fulfilment.

Divorced now for three years and with no children or grandchildren to dote on, Jane had been filling her time reading voraciously. Last summer her garden occupied much of her time but it was still too early to do much of anything in that regard, the Canadian winters being so bloody long and harsh.

Jane's one venture into the dating pool had been a flop.

She had met a nice man at a choral society practice and dated him for two months last fall. William was a fascinating conversationalist and most charming, highly refined and always meticulously dressed.

Also divorced with no children, he seemed like a promising candidate for a possible long term relationship. In fact William, who adamantly refused to be called Bill, appeared almost perfect.

Always a bit of a cynic, Jane chastised herself mildly for not realizing early on that William was too good to be true.

They had been dating for more than a month when Jane began to wonder why William had never shown her his apartment.

For the next three weeks, despite hinting unsuccessfully several times that she would love to see his place, no tour was forthcoming. Jane had begun to think the worst. Could William be like Norman Bates, living in his apartment with his dead mother perched on a rocking chair?

Finally, after taking in an early movie one Saturday evening, Jane pressed the issue and insisted on seeing William's digs.

The result was even worse than discovering a beloved deceased mother rotting away in her rocker.

A reluctant William nervously unlocked his apartment door and held it open for Jane to enter.

It was horrible.

On the carpet just in front of her as she stepped inside was a large dollop of fresh cat vomit. The place reeked with a variety of obscene odors.

A small army of cats eyed Jane suspiciously. Some were lounging on the sofas, two more were resting on the dining-room table and another was actually on the kitchen counter.

Jane spotted more felines sitting on William's bed in what was obviously his bedroom, and the spare bedroom was used solely as a kitty toilet area with litter trays scattered throughout the room.

Uncovered cat feces spread their obnoxious smells throughout the entire apartment.

A deeply embarrassed William mumbled, "I'm so sorry for the state of the place, Jane. I wasn't expecting company. Does it smell a bit in here?"

"A bit! It's abominable! You never mentioned that you were a cat fanatic. How can you even live in this stench?"

"I can't really smell anything. I suppose I've grown accustomed to it. They're my babies but it wasn't totally by choice. I do love animals and had two cats of my own. A couple of summers ago I noticed a stray cat out back so I put down a bit of food. A moment later there were three kittens eating with the mother cat, and it transpired that the mother was already pregnant with what turned out to be three more kittens a couple of months later. It took me a while, but I tamed all the kittens and the mother. As a result I'm now stuck with nine cats. I've bonded with all of them."

At that moment Jane had begun to sneeze uncontrollably and William had driven her home.

"How can you live in that filthy, unhealthy environment but dress and act so immaculately in public?" Jane had asked incredulously.

William had no satisfactory answer.

Although she went out with him twice more, the magic had disappeared. Jane declined any further dates and dropped out of the choral society to avoid running into the cat freak.

No other romantic prospects had surfaced since then, a fact which Jane found rather depressing.

This current search for answers about Ronald and Sonia had reignited Jane's former zest for life and she was greatly anticipating her upcoming excursion to America.

CHAPTER 23 (Alien Surveillance)

The two alien creatures had always existed together in some type of confined space. They had no inkling how they got there or when but somehow they knew that their names were Jarlon and Larjon.

They communicated by sharing their thoughts but had no particular physical shape. They could be more accurately described as wisps of smoke.

One day while they were in a dormant phase roughly akin to sleeping, two toys had appeared like magic to greet them when they awoke.

These toys were in fact two identical parallel worlds and for a long period of time the creatures took delight in observing their respective toys. By using their thoughts, the creatures were able to call up specific locations in those worlds and watch the activities on each of the two screens.

By chance they eventually zeroed in on Chicago and selected a human female named Sonia Poniecki to be their main source of vicarious amusement.

Jarlon quickly became bored. Having these new toys to observe was certainly preferable to having no stimulation except each other, but a craving permeated its being to compete with Larjon. Jarlon began experimenting and discovered that it was able to spin itself off into one of the life forms inside its own toy. Larjon had no such ability.

Eventually Jarlon felt a deep need to make his toy different from Larjon's.

Shortly thereafter, Jarlon spun itself off into a human male, entered its own world, and exterminated Sonia Poniecki on December 12th, 2014.

Larjon had been furious when Jarlon later explained what it had done to initiate tiny changes between the two formerly identical toys.

For the next three months, the differences had been minor and predictable.

Inexplicably, beginning on March 25th, 2015 the two worlds began experiencing rapidly escalating variations from each other.

Neither creature was able to solve the problem because both of them were focusing on Sonia Poniecki.

Finally on May 14th, 2015 Jarlon discovered the paradox in the lives of Ronald Smith. The creature had never thought to delve into that human male's life in his own world. Sonia's boyfriend shouldn't even have existed in Larjon's world. Smith should have remained in the coma just as his counterpart in Jarlon's toy had done.

That epiphany changed everything and explained why the differences between the two worlds had mushroomed out of control. They hadn't been caused by Sonia Poniecki's removal. Instead, Ronald Smith's continued existence in Larjon's world had been the trigger for the exponential differences.

At the time of his epiphany, Jarlon had already decided to enter Larjon's world in order to exterminate Sonia Poniecki, believing at the time that her removal would bring the experiment under control.

Once Jarlon pinpointed the problem as being caused by Ronald Smith and began to track him, another inexplicable puzzle was discovered.

The human male no longer could be found in Larjon's world but apparently had transported into Jarlon's toy.

Jarlon was unable to track Ronald Smith but did locate him posing as Donald Smith in the apartment in Laughlin.

Jarlon amended its plan, choosing to enter its own toy first, kill the imposter Smith and then enter Larjon's toy in order to terminate Sonia Poniecki.

Unfortunately, when Jarlon's spinoff was reunited with Jarlon after its physical entry into the two worlds, the results had been entirely negative.

The initial failure was the absence of Donald Smith in the apartment previously occupied by Ronald Smith. The probability of Smith's escape being coincidental was statistically impossible. Somehow Smith had been forewarned of Jarlon's coming.

As if the failed termination of Smith wasn't enough of a setback, his continued existence in Jarlon's world would inevitably cause uncontrolled changes, the extent of which would result in a gradual reduction of Jarlon's ability to spin itself off into physical beings and manipulate events.

The next phase of Jarlon's incursion was even more disrupting. By the time its spinoff had successfully slipped into Lorjan's realm, Sonia Poniecki had also escaped and was untraceable.

Since the woman no longer showed up on either creature's radar, it was apparent that some unknown variable was at work causing these enormous upheavals in both worlds.

The inescapable conclusion was that Sonia Poniecki had also been transported into Jarlon's world.

That meant that neither Smith nor Poniecki could be tracked since the creatures' viewing radar wasn't transferable from one realm to another.

Jarlon had also discovered that its spinoff could only be maintained in either sphere for a limited amount of time.

Logic dictated that patience and vigilance would be required in order to locate and exterminate the two foreign presences now in Jarlon's world.

Jarlon suspected that it must have been Lorjan who had somehow forewarned the two humans. No other explanation seemed possible.

Absolutely no trace of either target was detected until February 17th, 2016 when Jarlon discovered that books authored by the two humans had just been released electronically in Jarlon's world.

Deeming it unsustainable to send a spinoff to Madison, Wisconsin for the length of time required to track down the two authors, Jarlon decided that its highest chance of success lay with monitoring the family of Sonia Poniecki in Chicago.

Those observations proved fruitless until March 2nd when Jarlon listened in to a conversation between Poniecki's mother and a woman named Jane Holland from Canada. That prompted Jarlon to begin monitoring Holland as well.

Two weeks later Holland appeared to have discovered that the targets resided somewhere near Monroe, Wisconsin and volunteered at the local food bank. Jarlon began watching that business also, confident that the elusive pair would soon be spotted.

The clandestine meeting in the doctor's building on Wednesday, March 23rd flew completely under Jarlon's radar, but that evening Jarlon was shocked to discover the details retroactively when Karen and Jeff Chandler went to Bernice's apartment and discussed what had transpired earlier that day.

A solid opportunity had been lost. The humans had proven to be more clever than anticipated.

Jarlon continued its surveillance of everyone who might lead to the actual location of Smith and Poniecki.

CHAPTER 24 (Meeting the Dead)

Jane took the shuttle bus to the main Toronto airport, obtained her boarding pass and waited for her flight to depart.

She had managed to pare down what she needed to bring into one carry-on bag plus an oversized purse.

The flight to Chicago was pleasant and Jane obtained her rental car without a hitch.

Torn between spending the night in Chicago in order to do a bit of sightseeing or driving immediately to Monroe, Jane opted for the latter.

Less than three hours later, Jane was checking into a motel in Monroe, Wisconsin. She freshened up and asked directions to the local food bank.

Of course, unbeknownst to Jane, Jarlon was monitoring her every move.

The food bank was quite busy when Jane arrived. She walked inside the building which served as both the warehouse and office.

A woman asked if she could help.

"Yes, thank you, I'm in town for a couple of days and hoped I'd run into Ronald and Sonia Smith. Are they by chance working today?"

The lady went to a posted work schedule list, scanned it and answered, "No, they've been off for the past three weeks but will be returning to duty next Thursday."

"That's a shame. They don't have a telephone and the only address I have is Rural Route 2, Monroe. Is there anyone who can provide me with directions to their home?"

"Follow me, ma'am. Barry Symons is volunteering today and he's friends with Ron."

When they found Barry, he was wearing a novelty T-shirt with the motto "LAWYERS ARE SCUM." Jane didn't have the nerve to ask the man why he hated attorneys.

Barry was very helpful and provided explicit directions to Jane.

She drove to the house and continued down the winding dirt driveway where she parked in front of the modest wooden home.

Jane got out of the car and knocked on the front door.

A woman answered and Jane's heart skipped a beat when she realized that this was indeed Sonia Poniecki.

"Hello, Sonia. I'm Jane Holland from Canada. Forgive my brazen intrusion, but I was absolutely fascinated when I read your books."

Sonia's warm smile vanished and an expression of concern and alarm filled her face. Nevertheless, she played the gracious hostess.

"Please come in and I'll fetch Ron."

Jane waited on the couch until Ron and Sonia emerged a couple of minutes later.

...

Sonia had apprised me of this surprise visitor. When we walked together into the living-room, I began the conversation.

"Forgive our shock, Jane, but you're the first visitor other than our landlord that Sonia and I have had since we moved in here last May. Do you mind telling us how you managed to find us?"

"I guess I'll start by admitting to having a one-track stubborn mind. I read your books

163

and found them to be astoundingly imaginative, but what aroused my curiosity was the strange claim in the second book that the events described were true, not fictional. I began to investigate the details contained in that book and verified with Florence Clarke in Durant, Oklahoma that a woman named Kate had indeed stayed there, exactly as portrayed in the book. I sent a copy of Sonia Poniecki's obituary photo to Flo who confirmed that Kate was either Sonia's identical twin or Sonia herself."

"Are you saying that you actually believe the book is true?" Sonia blurted.

"Not precisely, but it was obvious that some of the events did actually happen. I concluded that using real names and mixing them in with some verifiable facts might be just a clever marketing ploy."

"That doesn't explain how you discovered that we live in Monroe," I interjected.

"That piece of information was more difficult to uncover. I spoke with Helen Kirkwood, your publisher, and with several other characters named in your books, and they told me where their copies of the books had been mailed from. Then I began checking newspapers in this general area and stumbled upon your food bank picture in the local community newspaper."

"Whom exactly did you call?" Sonia queried.

"Ben Van Huizen in Belleville, where I now live, confirmed that he worked in the same legal building with Ronald Smith for many years, and that he had spoken with Donald Smith after Ron passed away in Laughlin. Peter Long verified that he had actually met both Don and Ron, and that they were identical twins. I had a nice chat with Sonia's mother in Chicago."

"When did you call Bernice?" Sonia interrupted.

"I called her on March 2nd."

"Well, at least that mystery is solved. Bernice asked me if I knew Jane Holland from Canada. I didn't connect the names until this moment."

A surprised Jane blurted out, "Are you saying that you've spoken with Bernice since I called her?"

"I'm reluctant to disclose any information, Jane. Look, Ron and I need to absorb the import of your presence in Monroe and discuss the ramifications. Would you like to come back later and have supper with us, say about six o'clock?"

"I'd love to. Please forgive me for intruding on your privacy. I assure you that I'm totally discreet. If you and Ron decide that you want me to keep what I've discovered completely to myself, I'm perfectly willing to oblige. I'll return at six o'clock. Is there anything you'd like me to bring?"

"Are you keeping notes?" I asked.

"Yes, I've got a detailed chronology of what I've done in a folder in the rental car. Would you like me to leave it with you now?"

"Yes, that would be most helpful. Sonia and I need to determine whether your presence might constitute a real threat to us and to you. We'll see you at six o'clock."

Jane retrieved the folder from the car and handed it to Sonia, promising to return at the agreed time and that she would bring along a bottle of wine.

CHAPTER 25 (Rating the Danger)

As our unexpected visitor drove away, Sonia carried the folder back into the house and handed it to me.

"Let's read the material before we start to panic, honey," she suggested.

I studied Jane's notes while Sonia set the table for supper. This would constitute the first time we'd had a dinner guest, and Sonia admitted that she was greatly looking forward to the company, especially someone with whom Sonia could discuss the exceedingly strange life we'd been leading.

By the time Sonia had decided what to cook for supper and had done the initial preparations, I had finished perusing the entire folder. I handed it to Sonia who sat down and began reading.

When she too had glanced over everything in the folder, it was time to put dinner in the oven. When that task was done, we sat down in the living-room.

"Jane is quite the little detective," I began. "If she was able to find us, do you think the creatures can be far behind?"

"They didn't catch us at Bernice's doctor's office, so my guess is that they're not so powerful after all. It's likely that enough time has elapsed and they've given up. Even more probable, by now we may have caused enough changes between this world and our old one that the creatures no longer have the ability to interfere with either world."

"I tend to agree. How candid do you think we should be with Jane?"

"I'm going to enjoy discussing our situation with her in gory detail," Sonia answered. "As far as I'm concerned, the more folks who know the truth, the better off this world and our old world will be."

"What if Jane's discoveries do lead the creatures right to our door?"

"I don't think I have it in me to pack up and go underground again, Ron. We're happy here and the money seems to be holding up rather well. If the creatures did show up, I'd rather stand and fight them."

"I'm sure we wouldn't stand a chance. I've got no fighting skills at all. The most we can hope for is that Cecil or Old Ron would give us a bit of warning. Cecil was able to contact us through our dreams but he was convinced that some higher power was permitting him to do so. We'll have to hope that the same superior entity will do whatever's necessary to protect us."

"If we are attacked, is there anything we can use to defend ourselves?" Sonia asked.

"I'll check around the garage and the cellar."

I went down to the basement to ascertain what potential weapons were available. Ted Perlberg had left practically everything intact and had removed only his mother's valuables before leasing the house to us.

An old axe was the only weapon I could find. I brought it upstairs and showed Sonia.

We decided to put the axe in the kitchen broom closet to provide us with at least the illusion that we could protect ourselves from an intruder, alien or otherwise.

"I wonder if we should try to purchase a gun," Sonia queried.

"I don't even know how to use one and I doubt that Old Ron did either. If he was skilled in firearms, I'd have retained that general knowledge, but I don't think I even know which end the bullet shoots out of. You're American. Have you ever fired a gun?"

"Of course I have. Dad taught me when I was a teenager, and we always kept a firearm in the house when I was married to Allan."

"Well, I guess we can look into purchasing a gun somewhere. It would be too risky to provide our identification to a gun shop. Do you know any way to buy one on the sly?"

"We might be able to pick one up at a flea market. There's an outdoor bazaar every Sunday in the parking lot of the Northway Mall. I'd certainly feel safer knowing that we were well protected."

"What are your thoughts about Jane?" I asked. "She could blow our cover at any time. Do you think we can trust her?"

"It's probably too late anyway. She's already found us. I wish now that we hadn't posed for that volunteer banquet picture. It's quite unsettling to realize how much information is out there on the internet. Look, Jane will be here shortly. We'd better clean up and put on something nicer. She's our first dinner guest and I'm looking forward to her company."

CHAPTER 26 (Elimination Plans)

"This would appear finally to be our optimum opportunity to salvage our toys," Jarlon declared. "Have you reconsidered your willingness to assist with my departure?"

"I won't be partaking in your continuing folly, Jarlon. Your lack of ethics continues to appall me. Killing innocent life forms for casual experiment is wrong no matter how limited their intelligence."

"Utilize your intellect, Lorjan. There are many billions of humans milling around in each realm, killing each other over the most inane provocations or societal differences. I'm doing them all a favor by exterminating two insignificant individuals. I would greatly appreciate your assistance this time."

"I absolutely refuse. You failed even to inform me before you propelled your spinoff into its previous heinous assignments. Imagine my delight when you reluctantly disclosed that your most recent presumptuous insertion into my world was an utter failure. You had no right to tamper with my toy in any way without my permission. To discover that your mission involved the intended murder of an innocent creature in my realm is unforgiveable. Not only do I refuse to assist you now, but I also intend to thwart and disrupt your plans if the opportunity presents itself."

Jarlon sizzled with anger.

"I knew it was you who warned the Poniecki woman in your realm. No other explanation was logical."

A confused Lorjan attempted to conceal its surprise. Lorjan had been completely unaware of Jarlon's trespass until after it had taken place. Realizing that it had a greater chance of ruining Jarlon's current despicable plot by playing along and gathering information, Lorjan asked. "Since you didn't need me before, why are you even seeking my assistance this time?"

"The logistics could be more problematical. I've discovered that my spinoff is severely restricted by whatever form it mimics, and its mental acuity is also obscenely impacted."

"You never disclosed such matters to me. Why do you foresee complications on this occasion?"

"Each successive spinoff appears to weaken my abilities. My intention this time is to exterminate Ronald Smith and Sonia Poniecki, but I haven't determined what to do about the Holland woman. I welcome your input."

"My recommendation would be to abandon your scheme altogether. Why does the prospect of annihilating one additional human even play into your diabolical equation?"

"My spinoff's power deteriorates rather quickly as its time spent in my toy increases. It may not be possible for my spinoff to deal successfully with three targets at once."

"Can't you appear in a superior form?"

"Like what?"

"Have your spinoff mimic something powerful like a large grizzly bear."

"The physical attributes would be sufficient, but the mental limitations would be highly unsuitable. A powerful but primitive spinoff could be distracted by the simple odor of food and rush into the kitchen to feast, thereby permitting the humans to escape."

170

"I believe I understand your limitations, but I repeat my adamant refusal to assist you in any manner."

"I urge you to reconsider. If the presence of Smith and Poniecki continues in my world, then any control we have over events in either world will erode. Even our ability to observe the toys might come to an end. Would you even chance the possibility that our toys would be taken from us? We'd be thrown back into our former existence consisting of nothing but each other. It is clearly in your own best interest to cooperate with me in order to prevent such a devastating outcome."

"I disagree. Your murder of the Poniecki woman in your toy was evil and I refuse to participate in another such deplorable action. Losing my privilege to observe my realm would be a punishment I am willing to accept."

"Your lack of self-worth disgusts me," Jarlon spat.

An angry Jarlon remained skeptical of the ability of its spinoff to successfully kill three human targets at once. Since terminating the Holland woman would create additional unforeseen differences between the two worlds, Jarlon decided to spare her life.

In order to do so, Jarlon needed to gauge the timing of the spinoff's transport so that it arrived in the living-room section of the residence long after the Holland woman had departed.

Jarlon chose the form of a huge and formidable male human specimen.

CHAPTER 27 (The Last Supper)

Sonia and I were sitting outside on lawn chairs when Jane arrived as agreed at six o'clock.

Jane handed me a bottle of white wine and a bottle of champagne.

I put the champagne in the refrigerator and we all sat in the living-room where I cracked open the white wine.

"Sonia and I were most impressed with your tenacity and investigative skills in finding us," I grinned. "What prompted you to spend the time required to get to the bottom of our mystery?"

"Tedium with my uneventful routine in Canada was the biggest factor. When I retired from banking in England and moved to Ontario to be near my mother, I had fantasies that a whole new life would unfold. That hadn't materialized. When I read your books and examined your claim that the story was true, an overwhelming urge came over me to use my brain and training for a change and investigate your seemingly preposterous allegations."

"What type of work did you do in banking?" Sonia inquired.

"I was a bank fraud investigator during my final seventeen years in England."

"That's interesting," Sonia replied. "I was in charge of the fraud division for a title insurance company in Chicago before I retired. You look too young to be retired."

"I'll turn sixty in April," Jane admitted.

"We're almost the same age," Sonia grinned. "I met Ron last year the day before my sixtieth birthday, and I invited him to my birthday party. Little did I know then that we'd be transported into some parallel world where we'd have to flee from alien assassins."

"Is there anything at all fictional in the books?" Jane asked.

"No," I interjected. "Sonia and I decided to make our stories as accurate as possible. Our goal was and still is to try to create as much positive change as we can in this realm. That's why we've been spending so much time volunteering at the food bank and participating in so many church projects. It spooked us when you drove up earlier today because we realized that our cover has finally been blown."

"I sincerely pray that I haven't put you in any danger."

"Sonia and I discussed the situation after we read your notes. We're almost convinced that the creatures have given up. It's possible that sufficient alterations have already occurred such that the ability of the aliens to interfere with events in both worlds has been shattered. At least that's our hope."

Sonia chirped in.

"Having said that, after you left earlier, Ron and I scoured around the basement and garage looking for any weapons we could use to defend ourselves. The only thing we found was an axe which we put in the kitchen broom closet."

I added, "Whether an axe would be effective is an entirely different obstacle. We have no idea how the aliens murdered Sonia in this world. According to the newspaper reports, they made it look like a vicious mugging but there were no witnesses. Cecil disclosed in our shared dreams that the creature named

173

Jarlon was about to enter each world to kill us, but Cecil also described them as shapeless apparitions. We assume that Jarlon has to take some physical form in order to enter this realm. If that's correct, then the axe may be of assistance. We would have preferred a gun and in fact we intend to purchase one if possible."

Dinner was a most enjoyable affair.

Sonia and Jane bonded amazingly and over the course of the meal, Sonia and I described in detail our itinerary from San Antonio, Texas all the way north to Monroe, Wisconsin. We also told Jane about our quiet and downscale life since arriving here.

When dessert was finally finished, Sonia suggested that Jane stay the night in the spare bedroom.

"That way we can open the bottle of champagne and continue the festivities," Sonia giggled. "I'm having a marvelous time."

"Thank you, Sonia. That's a wonderful idea! I've even got my belongings in the trunk of the car. I was a bit leery of leaving my small overnight bag in the motel room."

While Jane retrieved her bag, Sonia tidied up the spare bedroom.

I popped open the champagne and the party continued.

Just after midnight, the last bit of the champagne was poured into our glasses. Sonia inquired whether another bottle of wine should be opened, but the consensus was that enough alcohol had been consumed.

We prepared for bed, totally oblivious to the mortal danger that would soon befall us.

CHAPTER 28 (Murderous Intrusion)

Jarlon selected a human to clone into the spinoff, an unusually large specimen weighing almost 350 pounds who was serving life without possibility of parole in a Wisconsin state prison west of Milwaukee.

James "The Beast" Corbett was only thirty years of age but had spent more than two-thirds of his adult life behind bars. His latest crimes had shown an escalating propensity for violence and the system gave up on his chances of eventual rehabilitation. The last Judge had convicted Corbett of murder and the prison system had effectively thrown away the key.

While creating the spinoff, Jarlon was unable to monitor any portion of the world other than Corbett's prison cell.

Just before two o'clock in the morning, the spinoff, which was clothed in an orange prison jumpsuit, was transported successfully into the living-room of the small bungalow in Monroe.

Jarlon flexed its muscles and stretched in an attempt to gauge the power and coordination of this spinoff form. Satisfied that it could carry out the dual termination of Smith and Poniecki quickly and efficiently, Jarlon walked softly toward the targets' closed bedroom door.

The movement of the bulky form caused a bit of creaking in the floorboards.

...

I was startled awake, aware of someone in the living-room.

Relax, I thought, it's just Jane getting up to use the bathroom.

Then I heard our bedroom doorknob turning quietly. I nudged Sonia and quickly sat up, alert and apprehensive.

Some moonlight filtered through our window and very slightly illuminated the room.

Sonia also sat up and her breathing was heavy. I realized that she too was anxious.

She called out, "Jane, is that you?"

Suddenly the bedroom door flew open and a giant clad in orange stood menacingly just inside the doorway.

I yelled to Sonia to run but before she could get out of our bed, a massive fist slammed into her and knocked my darling onto the floor.

The intruder turned his attention on me and lunged. I attempted to slow him down by throwing the blankets and sheets in front of me. He did get tangled up in the bedding but that didn't prevent him from falling on me.

His bulk was crushing and he was trying to free his hands. I used Sonia's pillow to shield my face from the brunt of his rain of powerful blows.

As a result I couldn't see a thing but prayed that Sonia and Jane could escape during the short period it would take for this brute to kill me.

My mind was buzzing with questions about whether the creatures had found us or if this was just your routine Saturday night American home invasion.

Both my arms were pinned under the pillow in a futile defensive posture to protect myself. I felt absolutely helpless and could hear Sonia moaning nearby. She hadn't been able to leave the room.

Despite the sheet and blankets, I managed to wrap my legs around the intruder in a feeble attempt to postpone my inevitable demise long enough for Sonia to get up and flee.

We were doomed.

…

Meanwhile, Jane had fallen asleep quickly and completely. The bed was extremely comfortable and in her dreams she heard creaking. The next thing she knew, Sonia was calling out to her. Jane woke up.

The next few moments were terrifying.

Jane heard Ron yelling followed by the chilling noises of a fight.

Jane leapt up and opened her bedroom door. She ran to the kitchen, switched on the light and found the axe in the broom closet.

Then she scurried into the main bedroom and switched on that light. Sonia was on the floor beside the bed and a huge man dressed in orange clothing was sitting atop of and beating on Ron.

Jane hoisted the axe above her head and brought it crashing down on the back of the attacker. That elicited the most eerie sound she had ever heard, something akin to the howl of a primitive beast.

Determined to save her friends and herself, Jane raised the axe high above her head and swung it with all her strength. By this time the orange brute had turned his attention to Jane and was attempting to extricate himself from the bedding and Ron's legs.

The axe blade drove into the huge left arm of the invader and elicited another savage growling response.

Ron was still helpless but Sonia had managed to stand up. She picked up a lamp and crashed it down on the back of the attacker's head. That further distracted him and he knocked Sonia back onto the floor with a powerful backhand blow.

This momentary distraction gave Jane the opportunity to hoist the axe once more. She plunged the blade deeply into the assailant's shoulder near his neck.

As he swiveled around, the axe remained imbedded and was torn from Jane's grasp.

The giant appeared confused as he scrabbled off the bed and stood upright.

...

All three of us were frozen in place staring at this seemingly invincible behemoth.

We had given it our best shots but to no avail. He was still going to murder us.

The intruder took a step toward Jane. I dragged myself into a standing position on the bed and flung myself onto the attacker's back.

In his weakened state, the force of my jump caused our adversary to collapse onto the floor. I rained a series of punches to the sides of his head as a glimmer of hope flickered in my mind. Perhaps the three of us had been successful after all in repelling this vicious home invasion.

I heard Jane call in the emergency on her cell phone. My fists were already throbbing but I continued to throw my best shots at the assailant's head.

Suddenly the attacker vanished into thin air and my punch scraped against the floor.

Sonia, Jane and I were stunned speechless.

"What just happened?" Sonia finally stammered.

"I can't explain it," I replied confusedly.

"Everything you've been writing about is true," Jane exclaimed. "The creatures must have sent this thing to kill you and now they've called it back to their world."

Exhausted and incredibly sore, I sat down on the bed, stupefied that we were still alive.

A siren blaring in the distance quickly got louder as help approached.

Sonia stumbled into the living-room and unlocked the front door just as the police barreled into our front yard.

A single police officer, gun drawn, exited the squad car and entered the house. He followed Sonia and Jane into the bedroom where I still sat in sheer bewilderment and exhaustion.

"Where's the intruder?" the cop inquired.

"He vanished," Sonia answered.

"What do you mean? Did he get away?"

"Sort of," I replied. "He literally disappeared while I was perched on his back with this axe buried in his shoulder."

The officer was more than skeptical as he surveyed the room. "Whose blood is this?" he barked.

Sonia answered. "It's the attacker's blood."

The cop asked us to raise our arms and he examined each of us for wounds. The right side of Sonia's face was already beginning to swell up and it was apparent that she had been struck. My fists were bruised, red and bleeding slightly.

The police officer looked at me suspiciously. "Are you sure you didn't strike your wife? Is this your blood on the floor?"

Jane spoke up forcefully. "Use your brain, officer. The volume of blood on the floor is substantially more than could possibly result from the tiny scrapes on Mr. Smith's fist."

"Let's start over, folks. I'm Officer Brian Williams. Please identify yourselves and then you can tell me exactly what occurred here. The 911 call indicated that a home invasion was in progress."

"I'm Ronald Smith and this is my wife Sonia. The other lady is our houseguest, Jane Holland. I awoke to the sound of creaking floorboards and then heard someone turning the doorknob to this room. I woke Sonia up. A huge man dressed in orange attacked me while I was in the bed."

I described the rest of the fight as accurately as I could recall. Sonia and Jane jumped in from time to time to clarify or expand on what I said since each of us had witnessed the incident from a different vantage point.

Officer Williams listened intently and said nothing. He called the precinct, briefly explained what had happened and requested that they send someone from forensics immediately.

Then he took a closer look at the bloody axe and the blood on the floor.

"Each of you claims to have gotten a good look at the intruder. It seems obvious that he was wearing a prison uniform, and from your descriptions, the man must be at least six and a half feet tall and well over 300 pounds. Do you think you could identify him from mug shots?"

We all answered in the affirmative.

"I'll have a forensic team here shortly and they can dust for fingerprints and take a sample of the intruder's blood. I believe I understand what occurred here tonight except for how the attacker escaped. Are you sure you weren't so terrified that he simply ran off?"

"No," I insisted. "He vanished like a puff of smoke right before our eyes. When I jumped on his back, he fell to the floor and disappeared while I was hitting him."

Williams checked the doors and windows for signs of forced entry and tried to discredit our firm recollections that the doors and windows were all locked when we went to bed.

The forensic team arrived and consisted of one female officer, Sergeant Fran Beckingham, who seemed disgruntled to have been summoned in the middle of the night. She had no trouble finding fingerprints on the bedroom doorknob. She photographed them and emailed them to the precinct.

While she and Officer Williams were still in the house, Beckingham received a positive response on her smart phone. The attacker was in the system. His name was James "The Beast" Corbett and he was currently an inmate at the state prison in Watertown west of Milwaukee.

Beckingham showed us a mug shot on her device and all three of us positively identified Corbett as the home invader. The Sergeant called the precinct to advise that Corbett had been positively identified as the home invader, but thereupon she got into a somewhat heated argument with the person on the other end of the line. She ended the call angrily by almost shouting, "That's not possible. I'll bring the damn blood to the station right now so it can be compared with Corbett's for type and DNA. It's fresh from the crime scene. I tell you, Corbett can't be safe in his cell. He couldn't have made it from here to there by now."

She spoke with Williams and they asked the three of us to attend at the precinct later in the morning at eleven o'clock to give formal statements. Beckingham didn't disclose the details of her phone call but we certainly got the gist of it from what she had said.

Officer Williams asked if we thought it was wise to remain in the home with the intruder still at large.

"Ron and I will definitely stay here," Sonia declared. "Jane, would you rather go to your motel room now?"

"I'd never be able to sleep. If it's okay with you, Sonia, I'd much rather stay here and talk about what happened."

"Of course it's acceptable. I'll put on some coffee. Thank you, officers for your swift response and your concern for our safety. We'll be at the police station promptly at eleven."

Beckingham took a few more pictures of the bedroom and the blood stains on the floor and advised that she was finished if Sonia wanted to clean the room before the stains set. She put the axe in an evidence bag and then both she and Officer Williams departed.

CHAPTER 29 (Restricted Disclosure)

When the police left, Sonia and Jane cleaned the floor and removed the bedding while I showered and dressed.

Later, over coffee and toast, we discussed our frightening ordeal.

"What did you make of Sergeant Beckingham's call to the precinct?" Jane asked.

"It sounded as if Corbett was securely in his prison cell all night despite his fingerprints being on our bedroom doorknob," I answered. "It will be interesting to know whether the blood on our floor also matches Corbett's."

Sonia chimed in. "I wonder if the Corbett in the prison will have fresh wounds on his back and shoulder."

"That would certainly confuse the police," Jane responded. "I guess we can't blame them, but they just couldn't wrap their minds around our claim that Corbett vanished into thin air."

Sonia gasped. "It just dawned on me, Jane. You saved all of our lives by grabbing the axe and hacking that brute. You must have been terrified."

"My mind was too focused on stopping Corbett from killing Ron. I don't think I felt any fear. How much of your story do you think you'll divulge to the police?"

"They don't seem capable of thinking outside the box," Sonia answered. "There's no way they'll believe our claim to be from a parallel world or that alien creatures are trying to kill us."

I interjected. "Unanswerable questions will also arise if the police check into our own identities. The only type of alien I'll seem to them is the illegal variety even if they don't discover that I'm supposed to be dead. I'm a Canadian who has been living in Monroe for almost a year. They'll almost certainly deport me."

"I guess we'd best decide on a story and stick with it," Sonia suggested. "What are your thoughts, Jane?"

"I'm totally convinced that the truth of the matter is incomprehensible to most people, especially to the police who are trained to deal in verifiable facts. It requires an actual demonstration like what just occurred to convince anyone. I'll back up whatever version you choose to tell them."

We talked it over for a couple of hours and finally concluded that we wouldn't stray from the story we had already told Brian Williams. We'd say that Corbett or someone looking remarkably like him attacked us and seemed to vanish. We would let the police reach the conclusion that the intruder got away in the utter confusion of the moment.

The fact that we had been successful in thwarting the creatures' murderous attempt on our lives gave us some comfort. It appeared that Jarlon had to assume the form of an actual person, and therefore it was possible for us to defend ourselves. We weren't dealing with an omnipotent force after all like Cecil had hinted.

We were also gaining a slight confidence that perhaps no further alien assassins would appear in our new world.

Jane even offered up the possibility that God had intervened to prevent our murders. It was an enormous coincidence that Jane had become so interested in revealing the truth about us that she had left her home to come to Wisconsin on an investigative mission. As if that wasn't odd enough, Jane's unexpected overnight stay combined with our finding the axe as a potential weapon earlier on the same day did seem to hint at some form of divine intervention.

"Would you be willing to stay here at the house with us for another couple of nights?" Sonia asked Jane. "We'd certainly understand if you decline."

"Actually I'd feel safer here with the two of you rather than alone in a strange motel. I'll check out of the motel later when we go into town."

Jane drove us in to Monroe where she checked out of her room before we continued on to the police station.

Then the situation became somewhat complicated.

CHAPTER 30 (Strange Complications)

Sergeant Beckingham escorted us into a small interview room and handed us prepared witness statements.

"Please check these for accuracy and sign them if no changes need to be made. I've kept them brief."

Jane, Sonia and I carefully read our respective statements, confirmed that they were correct and duly signed them.

Then things got interesting.

Beckingham brought us up-to-date on the investigation.

"The blood on your floor definitely belongs to James Corbett, as do the fingerprints found on the bedroom entrance doorknob. The trouble is that Corbett was just as definitely locked securely in his prison cell during the entire home invasion. The prison tapes and statements from Corbett's cellmate irrefutably confirm same. In addition, Corbett has no wounds whatsoever on his body and his prison jump suit is undamaged. Can any of you explain that paradox?"

We all replied in the negative.

Calmly, Beckingham dropped her bombshell.

"I understand, Mr. and Mrs. Smith, that you are published authors."

The Sergeant reached into her briefcase and pulled out a Kindle E-Reader, tapped on it and showed us our second book, "ALIEN ASSASSINS ARE AFTER US."

"I've been feverishly attempting to finish your novel before you got here. I noticed copies of it in your living-room and on a bookshelf in the kitchen. I believe that I understand the gist of your theory, but it raises the disturbing possibility that this whole home invasion claim is nothing but an elaborate publicity stunt. I'm going to have to insist on seeing some identification."

Without any hint of the shock that permeated my entire being, I responded with the blankest of poker faces.

"I'm so sorry but you have no valid legal basis on which to compel your request. We've signed our statements and now we'll be heading home."

Beckingham turned to Jane. "Are you willing to show me your ID?"

"Of course," Jane responded as she pulled out her driver's license and Canadian passport.

"Are you aware of their book?"

"Yes, ma'am."

"Are you involved in the publication or promotion of the book?"

"No."

"Why were you visiting with Mr. and Mrs. Smith?"

"Before I decide whether to answer any further questions, I want to speak privately with Ron and Sonia."

"Very well, I'll leave the three of you alone for a few minutes. By the way, a gentleman from the Chicago police force will be arriving here at any moment now, and I'm afraid that none of you may leave until he determines whether some type of fraud has been committed."

Beckingham departed and closed the door on her way out.

"Good God," Sonia exclaimed. "What are we going to do, Ron?"

"I guess this is as good a time as any to disclose the whole truth and accept any and all consequences," I replied.

Jane asked, "Do I have your permission to answer truthfully any questions they ask me?"

"Of course you do," Sonia and I answered simultaneously.

A woman poked her head in and offered to get us coffee and food. We accepted and shortly thereafter coffee and doughnuts were delivered from a fast food outlet.

During the next hour the three of us discussed the possible outcomes of blurting out the entire truth as we knew it. We concluded that the matter was pretty much out of our control now.

Finally Beckingham returned with a large gentleman she introduced as Detective Larry Mitz from Chicago. He explained that he was the officer who had investigated the unsolved murder of a woman in Chicago in December of 2014. Two cardboard boxes were carried in, both labelled as "Sonia Poniecki murder investigation."

Sonia and I exchanged worried glances.

"Have you changed your mind about providing us with formal identification?" Beckingham barked.

"Yes," I replied. "Sonia and I have discussed the situation in some detail. We're going to leave it up to you to determine whether to keep what we tell you absolutely secret, which is the outcome we strongly recommend. Meaning no disrespect, Sergeant Beckingham, but we also believe it best if only Detective Mitz hears what we have to say. He can decide how much information to disclose to you. Is that acceptable?"

She looked quizzically at Mitz who pondered our request for a moment and then nodded.

"What about Ms. Holland?" Beckingham asked. "Do you want her to stay with you or come with me?"

Sonia answered. "Jane is part of the entire story so it's best if she remains."

Beckingham left after advising Mitz that he could call her on Extension 23 if he needed anything.

Mitz got right down to business.

"I downloaded a copy of your two books onto my E-Reader a few minutes ago but obviously haven't had a chance to read them. The Sergeant gave me a brief synopsis."

He turned to Sonia.

"You bear a remarkable resemblance to my murder victim. Can you explain that?"

Sonia reached into her purse and handed Mitz her driver's license from Illinois and her US passport, both documents still unexpired.

"Are you saying that you are Sonia Poniecki?"

"Yes sir."

"I saw you dead at the murder scene in Chicago and I've got pictures to prove it," he barked as he opened one of the cardboard boxes and extracted several photographs from an envelope.

Sonia gasped when she looked at them.

"These are photos from the crime scene and pictures from the subsequent autopsy which was performed on Sonia Poniecki, along with her signed Death Certificate. Do you still claim to be her?"

"Yes and no," Sonia responded. "I am Sonia Poniecki but I'm the identical version from a parallel world. You can take a DNA sample along with my fingerprints if you wish. It would probably be more efficient if you took a few hours to read the second book and met with us at our house this evening."

"I'll think about it." Mitz then turned to Jane. "What is your role in this matter?"

Jane explained about reading the books and being fascinated with the imaginative claim that the stories were true. She related how she had embarked on an investigative adventure which culminated last night in the almost deadly home invasion.

"Do you believe your friends?"

"I certainly do now. The attack by James Corbett was as real as sitting here now with you. As preposterous as their story sounds, it really did happen and you'll have to be the one to decide whether to bury the story or publicize it."

"Excuse me for a moment," Mitz muttered as he left the room.

A few minutes later he returned with Beckingham who proceeded to take DNA swabs from Sonia and me along with full sets of fingerprints.

When Beckingham had left the room, Mitz turned his attention on me. "What will I find out about you?"

I showed him my own ID.

"I'm also dead in this world. The Ronald Ward Smith here died in Laughlin, Ontario on May 14th last year. He was mugged by a couple of drugged-up thugs in March of that year and never awoke from a coma. In the parallel world from which Sonia and I were transported, I did emerge from the coma although with no memories of my previous life. The first book entitled 'FRUGAL LAWYER, FLASHY LAWYER' details my life in that other realm and my chance meeting with

Sonia. I was later transported involuntarily into this world where I discovered that Sonia was no longer alive. Sonia was also transported here shortly thereafter in order to escape the creatures seeking to kill her in that other world. Please read the books."

Mitz excused himself again and was absent for at least thirty minutes.

He returned with Sergeant Beckingham.

"Here's what we're going to do, folks. We're holding all of your pieces of identification for the moment. You're free to return to your home but an officer will be assigned to follow you. He will remain posted at your front door. Sergeant Beckingham and I will come around at six o'clock this evening and we can discuss this dog's breakfast then. In the meantime the Sergeant and I will pore over your books and try to confirm information about the other Ronald Smith. Is that acceptable?"

We agreed and Jane drove us back to the house.

CHAPTER 31 (An Imperfect Resolution)

Mitz and Beckingham arrived just after six o'clock and accepted Sonia's offer of coffee.

When the five of us had positioned ourselves around the kitchen table, Mitz brought us up-to-date.

"It's now been satisfactorily verified, folks. Both of you possess fingerprints identical to the deceased Sonia Poniecki and Ronald Smith. DNA comparisons won't be available for a week or two but I expect they'll match up perfectly also. I read both of your books but there's been no time to corroborate any of the information."

Jane piped up.

"Perhaps I can assist you in that regard. These are the detailed investigative notes I made including a full listing of the various details of the books that I was able to validate."

Jane then explained how she had narrowed down her search to the Monroe area and how she had finally spotted our pictures in the community newspaper.

Once Jane had finished, Sonia mentioned that we had in fact contacted Bernice and Karen face to face in Chicago on March 23rd just a few days ago.

Mitz reacted in surprise to that disclosure.

"Do I have your permission to call your mother and your daughter now to confirm what you've just told me?"

Sonia acquiesced and gave the telephone numbers to the Detective.

Mitz called Bernice first and allowed Sonia to speak with her when he was done. Sonia assured her mother that everything was fine and that it now appeared to be safe to resume regular and open contact.

Karen was somewhat less accepting of Sonia's reassurances but calmed down when Sonia promised that we would come to Chicago for a visit next week.

When Sonia handed the phone back to Mitz, he said, "Both your mother and daughter claim to believe your story and they verified that you did in fact contact them at the doctor's office. I don't know at this moment what to think about anything. What are your thoughts, Sergeant?"

"The whole idea is so creepy, strange creatures which are able to take the form of actual people and commit dreadful crimes. It's just too farfetched for me to even pretend to understand, let alone believe it's happened. What I do know is that I can't prepare an official report along those spooky lines which has any possibility of being credible. If nobody would believe us, then it seems senseless to put the supernatural aspect of the story on paper."

"I tend to agree," Mitz concurred. "I'm also concerned about the public's reaction if we do prepare a report based on what Ron and Sonia have told us, and somehow it gets leaked out. There might be uncontrollable panic."

"What are our options?" Beckingham asked.

Mitz appeared to be deep in thought for a few moments before answering.

"One possibility is just to leave the report as is, call it merely a failed attempt at a home invasion in which the perpetrator managed to escape empty-handed without seriously injuring anyone. We can insert our opinion that the blood and fingerprints of James Corbett appear to have been planted at the crime scene, presumably as some sort of revenge prank against him or possibly as a ruse to confuse the police."

"I like that choice," Beckingham exclaimed, "but what about the victim statements describing a brutal axe fight?"

"Who knows the details of those statements?" Mitz asked.

"Only the people in this room and Brian Williams, the first officer on the scene, have been privy to the particulars of the assault. Brian shouldn't be any problem. He's transferring to the Milwaukee police force in a couple of days. I brought the crime scene notes and the victims' signed statements with me tonight in case it became necessary to refer to them."

Beckingham retrieved the statements from a satchel and passed them around the room, asking each of us to comment.

I was the last one to read them.

"I've got an idea," I began. "If we cross out and replace the word 'axe' with the word 'broom', then the statements become fairly innocuous. The mention of Corbett's blood is a bit of a problem, but we can add a sentence that no one appeared to be cut in the scuffle and that the intruder must have poured out the blood from a container which he took with him when he fled. That would corroborate the assumption that the blood and fingerprints were planted by the assailant."

Everyone was in agreement with that strategy so the statements were doctored accordingly.

As the officers stood up to leave, I called Mitz aside.

"I think this course of action is prudent, Detective. No one would ever believe what we claim actually took place. Sonia and I are going to have an ongoing problem. I'm a Canadian and getting deported back to Canada would give rise to the same issues we discussed tonight. I'm dead in this world and so is Sonia. Unlike Sonia's surname, my last name is very common. To avoid future complications, we'll need some form of useable identification. Is there any way you might be able to assist us in that regard?"

Mitz pondered the matter for a moment and pulled out his smart phone. He jotted down a name and phone number and handed it to me.

"Call this number when you're in Chicago visiting Sonia's family next week. I'll give the guy a heads up, and he should be able to get you anything you'll need. He'll want a thousand bucks or so. Is that a problem?"

"No, sir, and we need to thank you so much for your understanding this evening. With any luck Sonia and I will be able to continue to blend in perfectly and live out normal lives in obscurity. If it turns out that we are murdered, then only you and Sergeant Beckingham will realize why the culprit vanished without a trace. Our fervent hope is that the creatures will give up in light of their recent failed attempt. We have no control over the situation unless we burrow underground again, and Sonia doesn't want to do that any longer. Reuniting with her family in this world is too important to her."

Mitz drove off with Sergeant Beckingham.

That evening Sonia, Jane and I discussed the imperfect resolution that had emerged from the indescribably complex situation.

Sonia and I began second-guessing what we'd agreed to, wondering if perhaps it would have been wiser to make the true story public. Doing so might have resulted in massive changes to this world and put a complete stop to the ability of the creatures to meddle in either realm. In the end we decided to take no further action.

...

Jarlon had recalled his spinoff just in the nick of time before the wounds inflicted by the targets and their unexpected overnight guest could have seriously impacted Jarlon itself.

Lorjan had witnessed the home invasion using Jarlon's toy. At first Lorjan had watched in horror, expecting the innocent humans to be savagely slaughtered.

As they valiantly and successfully defended themselves, Lorjan felt elation as Jarlon wailed out in agony and finally summoned his spinoff home. Justice had prevailed.

An angry and bitter Jarlon vowed that it would succeed on its next attempt, bragging that all that was required for a positive outcome was to select a human form expert in gunmanship and ensure that the spinoff was equipped with superior weapons. Jarlon also stated that it intended to terminate the Holland woman in both worlds.

"I will not rest until all three targets have been duly exterminated," Jarlon insisted. "Failure is not an option for me. I will simply observe faithfully and bide my time until the optimum opportunity presents itself. If their elimination results in the confiscation of our toys, then that is an unfortunate result I am willing to risk. Those humans have unwittingly issued a challenge to me which I wholeheartedly accept."

"I will do my utmost to prevent your vile project," Lorjan snarled in reply.

"But I shall nevertheless succeed," Jarlon hissed. "My superiority over you will eventually be proven conclusively."

...

Jane remained in Monroe as our house guest until her vacation came to an end. She and Sonia became great friends during that brief time.

The evening before Jane was to leave, the three of us had a fascinating conversation about how the recent events had affected our belief or non-belief in an afterlife and other God issues.

None of us had any particular belief in God, except that Sonia and Jane had been made to attend Sunday school and church in their younger days. That made it next to impossible for either of them to totally reject the notion of a higher power watching over mankind and judging conduct as worthy of Heaven or Hell.

Sonia hadn't thought deeply about such issues in decades, having concluded long ago that it was not possible to make any firm conclusions about those matters.

On the other hand, Jane had rejected the possibility of a loving God since she was horrified by the cruelty of humans, especially as related to their treatment of animals. The reality of factory farms in which cattle and chickens were raised in distressingly cramped stalls had convinced Jane that no caring God would have allowed such atrocities to continue.

My beliefs were uniquely nothing but a blank canvas since I had no recollection whatsoever about my past life that could influence my opinion now. I had read portions of the Christian Bible since emerging from the coma, hoping to gain some insight into religious belief, but found the Holy Book to be quite irrational in most places. The God as depicted in the Old Testament seemed cruel and arbitrary. The message in the New Testament was somewhat palatable but seemed totally unrealistic.

Those discussions led to more specific debates about our own situation.

I surmised that, "There must be at least some form of afterlife since Cecil was able to contact both Sonia and me in our dreams weeks after he died in his world. He admitted that he was conscious but appeared to be in some state of limbo."

"From what little I remember from Sunday school," Sonia interjected, "the concept of a parallel world seems pretty inconsistent with the whole creation story."

"There was certainly nothing in my religious education about malevolent creatures observing humanity and having the power to intervene in evil ways," Jane added. "It sort of debunks the idea that God made humans in His image."

"I can agree with both of your views," I replied, "but Cecil also mentioned that he felt that some higher power was providing him with the ability to eavesdrop on the creatures and contact Sonia and me through our dreams. I tend to believe that either God or some higher power was on our side and was instrumental in keeping us alive. Jane's presence with the handy axe in my view was much more than mere coincidence."

The only conclusions we reached were that each of us was determined to keep an open mind regarding such complicated matters, and that we hoped that God or whatever that higher power was, would continue to protect us in the event the creatures launched another attack. It seemed illogical that we'd be allowed to perish now after all we'd been through.

Jane drove us to Chicago on the morning of her flight departure. She dropped us off at Bernice's apartment where Sonia introduced Jane to Bernice. We had a nice chat before Jane had to leave for the airport.

Sonia and I had a wonderful visit with her family even though there was no way we could tell the truth to the grandchildren. We manufactured a story about Sonia working undercover for the CIA and swore the kids to secrecy. Sonia was ecstatic about the reunion and immensely relieved that she could now openly be a part of her family's life.

We obtained high quality fake ID from Detective Mitz's rather disreputable contact in Chicago. According to my new birth certificate and driver's license, I was now an American named Ronald Smith with no middle name, born in New York State.

Sonia Smith, also with no middle name, was my spouse, born in Texas as Sonia Gonzalez.

Back in Monroe a few days later, we purchased two handguns at a flea market and obtained a valid Wisconsin car license for our old rust bucket. Wisely, we obtained proper firearms instruction and practiced at a local firing range, since I had never fired a gun and Sonia hadn't done so since she was a young woman.

The following week we bought two smart phones and hooked them and our computers up to the internet.

Finally we opened a bank account at a Monroe credit union. We were back on the grid and would now be able to get jobs before our money ran out.

Jane Holland called Sonia in mid-April and Sonia put the call on speaker so that I could listen in. Jane had kept the events in Wisconsin completely to herself. She'd informed her mother that she had been unsuccessful in tracking down the authors but nevertheless had enjoyed her vacation.

Jane told us that she was somewhat fearful that her life might be in danger from the creatures, but that she had decided to go about her business and treat the threat the same way she viewed getting involved in a car accident. She would try to be vigilant but would entrust her future to the vagaries of fate.

Later that evening, Sonia and I agreed to adopt a similar attitude and try to live out our remaining days content in each other's company and deeply in love.

THE END